The Medallion
of Solaus

The Medallion of Solaus

Kimberly Adkins

Black Lyon Publishing, LLC

The Medallion of Solaus

Copyright © 2007 by Kimberly Adkins

Our books may be ordered through your local bookstore or by visiting:

www.BlackLyonPublishing.com

Black Lyon Publishing, LLC
PO Box 567
Baker City, OR 97814

This is a work of fiction. All of the characters, names, events, organizations and conversations in this novel are either the products of the author's vivid imagination or are used in a fictitious way for the purposes of this story.

Cover Model: Blue Winterhawk

ISBN-10: 0-9793252-3-4
ISBN-13: 978-0-9793252-3-6
Library of Congress Control Number: 2007929907

Written, published and printed in
the United States of America.

This book is dedicated to my cousin Ben.
I know you found your answers.

Prologue

She barely remembered the past few days. So many faces appeared before her, streaked with tears, eyes all reflecting the disbelief and sorrow her damaged soul stored deep inside. All she could really recall were those faces, their voices dampened as they spoke words of comfort. She felt some hid a hint of accusation behind their eyes.

"Kaitlin," she could hear faintly as someone gently patted her hand. "This wasn't your fault. He struggled with his own demons and wasn't able to overcome them. We all know you did everything you could for Alex."

Hearing his name was like a sharp, ringing slap to her face. Suddenly, vivid flashes of the past few days forced themselves from the back of her mind. She saw him lying there, face pale. She felt the horrifying sink of her heart as she realized he wasn't breathing.

It seemed an eternity before the paramedics came, and they told her later the CPR she performed on his still body may have extended his life for the few short days he lived afterward. All the years she fought through his depression to make their marriage work seemed like nothing as she watched his heart beat for the last time, just as helpless as she had always been to change his view of life.

The entire community was at the memorial. Alex and his

family were well loved by everyone who knew them, which is what made leaving him so difficult and what filled her with so much guilt as she stood by his family right now.

"It is not for us to understand why Alex took his own life," the minister spoke kindly to the gathering. "He is in the hands of God now, and we can take comfort in the fact that in the Kingdom of Heaven, he will finally understand the truth and see all the answers he was unable to find here with us."

She rarely prayed, but just this once, she squeezed her eyes tight and prayed to anyone who would listen that this would be true.

Chapter One

"Listen, Kaitlin," her publisher urged as they sat down together at the end of a long, black glossy conference table. "You're an award winning photo journalist. This is your art. This is what you do to express yourself. Just take a look around."

He gestured expansively at the frames hung about the meeting room. Stunning pictures of her magazine covers lined the walls. She regarded each one again, feeling the emotion they inspired not just within her but for the millions of others who felt that same joy as the child was pulled from the rubble of 9/11, or the heartache of the wife who just discovered her husband wasn't coming home from the War in Iraq.

"You haven't taken a single photo since Alex died," he reminded her softly. "Why don't you take this assignment? You're so fond of Egypt and the story is interesting to say the least. Take a few pictures, ease back into life such as we know it these days."

Kaitlin sighed, measuring his hopeful expression. He almost looked like an expectant puppy dog waiting to go for a walk. She respected her publisher a great deal; they'd worked closely together at the publication for many years and he'd always treated her with kindness. He was a good friend during her separation from Alex and a bastion of support in the weeks after his death.

She slowly turned away and looked at the skyline of the city through the window to take a moment to consider the offer.

Instead, she saw herself reflected in the tinted glass. She was a little surprised at the image there. A tired young woman with her long blond hair pulled back in a severe pony tail gazed back at her with swollen, red rimmed, blue eyes. How forlorn and lost this stranger seemed.

"You are stronger than this." Her publisher set a firm hand on her shoulder and whispered in her ear as the stranger in the reflection developed an almost defiant look on her face.

"Tell me about this assignment."

She spun around abruptly to face him. He grinned as if the sun had broken free of the heavy storm that had been raining on his parade for weeks.

"Well, my dear." He took her hand and leaned forward with a wink. "It involves a mysterious artifact, an unaccountable stranger and rumors of a lost treasure. I can't promise this contract will be without danger … "

She replied with a shadow of a smile. "It never is."

•

Kaitlin slipped cool, unbleached linen pants over her long shapely legs. She let a cream colored camisole slide gently over her arms as the supple silk fabric draped elegantly across her chest. She'd piled her thick, long hair on top of her head in the shower that morning and it was already beginning to come loose in rebellious tendrils around her face and shoulders.

Her taxi to the airport was late, but she hardly had room to complain as she grabbed a light jacket and her suitcase. The doorman helped her to the curb with her luggage just as the car pulled up. She slipped her hand inside her purse and came in contact with the padded envelope that supposedly contained the artifact her publisher had tempted her with the day before. Typical of her friend to have it delivered before she had a chance to examine it and change her mind.

"I'm right on time, Lady."

The driver grinned, assuming she'd been waiting for a while on the street. She didn't remark on his comment. The taxi ride would be a long one as Manhattan was probably the most difficult place to try to get to from the airport.

As they crawled into the traffic she opened her bag and reached inside for the paperback novel she'd picked up at an airport on another trip. The cover had an enticing picture of an Adonis-type man with his shirt off, muscles bulging as he ravished a helpless woman deep in the throes of ecstasy.

She smirked a little at the fictional pair, but her eyes were drawn to his lips pressed against the hollow of the woman's throat as his hand reached up her pale, smooth thigh. She felt a moment of breathless desire well up deep inside, an almost longing ache and she realized it had been a very long time since she felt anything like that in her reality.

"Ha!" She laughed out loud at her imagination.

The cabbie glanced at her briefly in the rear-view mirror and smiled in a somewhat disquieting manner. She was disturbed to notice the hot flush on her cheeks as well as the heavy breathing that had caused her chest to rise and fall rapidly.

Kaitlin felt a little violated during her private moment and gave the driver an icy glare. He shrugged nonchalantly and turned his eyes back to the road.

Slowly, she slipped the paperback into her bag again, brushing up against something inside. It felt very warm, almost alarmingly so and she pulled it free from her purse quickly. Though she was surprised it had worked itself free of the envelope, she knew immediately what it was.

There, wrapped in satin, was her key into a world most people knew very little about.

The society of treasure hunters, she thought to herself. An underground network built on the buying, selling and smuggling of ancient artifacts. Often the lowest members of the hierarchy didn't even know what they had. Many times a poor farmer would find a relic in a cave or some long lost tomb on his property and bring it into the city, selling it for enough money to feed his family for maybe a week. That item would change hands several times and progress up a line of buyers who would eventually sell it for what it was worth.

She carefully unwrapped the silken bindings and brought out the intricately engraved medallion. She ran her fingers over the smooth, dark golden metal, feeling the strange writing on the surface brush against the sensitive skin of her fingertips. It was so warm to the touch, she wondered if perhaps she had laid her purse in the hot summer sun in the cab.

Kaitlin was curious if the chain attached to the medallion was the original piece; it was surely very valuable if this were the case. The chain itself was woven in such an intriguing and unusual pattern that it was quite a prize on its own.

At that moment, she longed to put it on. She needed to feel that smooth metal against her skin. The warmth spread from the medallion through her fingertips and encased her entire body in a rush of exotic, tingling pleasure. She lifted it gingerly, beginning to raise the chain over her head.

"Lady!" the cab driver yelled a disturbing few inches from her face.

She suddenly became aware they were sitting in the departure zone at the airport and she was holding a priceless, not to mention probably illegal, artifact in full view of everyone in the area. Hastily, she rewrapped the object and apologized to the driver, murmuring something about losing track of the time as she returned it to her purse.

●

The plane was quite crowded, and although Kaitlin hadn't expected otherwise, she wished she could spend some private time inspecting the strange medallion her publisher had passed to her just before she called the taxi and began to pack.

She settled in as comfortably as she could for the long flight and went over what little of the plan they had for this assignment. It was a fairly simple task in theory, and part of her thought her associate was just sending her away in an attempt to take her mind off the past few weeks.

The medallion she carried was supposedly part of a collection of extremely unusual items found in a shipwreck off the coast of Alexandria, and it wasn't just the artifacts on board that were strange.

There was mention of a survivor along with the find, and it was actually this man who was heading up the classification and organization of all the contents. She wasn't sure how a lone person was able to survive a ruthless crew of treasure hunters and become the one in charge, and she wasn't sure if the shipwreck was old or new, but that was what made this all very interesting.

The publication had many freelance artists around the world, and it was one of these people who requested her personally. She was to come in as a hired professional to photograph this rare collection and leave.

The contact would get her inside the organization and both parties hoped to profit from the first run of pictures of a history-altering find should the relics prove to be valuable and important. It all sounded simple, though when dealing with the underground one could never feel completely safe and secure.

"Alright," she sighed to herself, pulling out the paperback again. "This is the only romance I'm likely to have in my life any time soon, so let's get to it."

The lights over the passengers dimmed as darkness came on. A soft and steady vibration from the plane's engines made her sleepy in the warm, crowded cabin. Her eyes became heavy and the book in her hand slowly closed to rest gently in her lap.

Kaitlin lay immobile as the heavy, enticing scent of sandalwood oil wafted through the cabin. In her half wakeful state, she couldn't tell if she was dreaming or if she actually smelled the intoxicating perfume.

Very slowly she began to relax. It was extremely dark and she almost felt as if she were lying down. Carefully, reverently, strong oiled fingers began to stroke the bare skin of her shoulders. She tried to raise her head, yet could do nothing except open her eyes very slightly.

For a moment Kaitlin panicked, but the scent around her made her dizzy and euphoric. She thought briefly of the captive woman on the cover of her book. If this was a dream, she decided she should take advantage of it.

Passion flooded her cheeks and she didn't try to resist the hands as they caressed her intimately. Torches crackled in their sconces. She could see the firelight flicker across her heavy lids, and smell the old-fashioned pitch and iron in the room. The figure looming over her was a mere shadow against the flames as he changed scents again to something she couldn't identify, and began anointing her chest.

She gasped with an overwhelming desire she'd never experienced in her life and as her lips parted, he brought forth one finger and delicately skimmed her lips with a sweet tasting gloss. Without control, she brushed her lips against his finger, gently licking the inside length with the tip of her tongue, longing to taste his skin.

His shadow loomed over her and he spoke in lush, beautiful tones.

"You are mine—forever."

"Yes," she breathlessly replied, straining with every fiber in her being to touch him again.

He brought his mouth onto hers with surprisingly brutal force, kissing her as if his very life hung in the balance. He then stood upright and she felt as if her soul was being drawn out of her body as he backed into the torch light.

A deep, heavy grinding sound began near her toes, and the vibration progressed along the cold stone slab where she lay inert. The last thing she saw as the lid to the sarcophagus fell into place was a single tear glistening on the shadow of his face, before she lapsed into a deep sleep.

●

She couldn't shake the dream she had on the plane. Her head was fuzzy and she felt a little disoriented as she exited Customs. The deep, dry Cairo heat slammed into her and all the way through her body as she stepped out of the airport. Immediately, delicate beads of sweat broke out on her forehead and she briefly sat her bag on the sidewalk at her feet so she could sweep her hair back up on top of her head. Many admiring glances came her way, and she smiled inwardly at the flattering attention.

In the instant both hands were wound up in her glossy locks, a small child darted in front of her, grabbing her purse and streaking through the throng of travelers gathered at the departure area.

She cried out, running after him, terrified she would lose the medallion not only because the assignment would fail but because she secretly felt it was important to her somehow. Her heart pounding, she burst through the crowd in time to see the child held tightly by a man sitting on his heels with his back to her. He spoke sternly to the boy, who handed the purse to him. He stood and turned to face her.

Kaitlin was instantly stunned by his deep blue eyes, so full of emotion in that moment. His black hair was thick and framed his strong facial features as his rugged jaw sported a sad smile. He reached forward with one hand, his tan muscles rippling underneath his sky-blue shirt.

"I am sorry, Miss," he said smoothly and eloquently.

Her heart skipped a beat at the sound of his voice. At once it seemed familiar yet exotic to her. She took his hand and he shook hers firmly. She felt a little weak in the knees at his touch and her hand tingled.

"The child is desperate to feed his family." He gestured to the boy who was still at his side, his head hanging low. "It is sad that someone so young should feel there is no other recourse. I have often wished, since coming to this city, that there were not so many who suffered here."

"Wishes are magic if you have three." She said the first thing that came into her mind, a sing-song phrase her mother used to say to her over and over again as she'd grown up. She grimaced a little at the seemingly childish chant.

He regarded her with a startled look, which turned pensive. He turned back to the child and folded some paper money into his pants pocket. The boy smiled brilliantly and ran away in a flash. Kaitlin was deeply moved by his actions and reached out to gently set her hand on his shoulder.

"You were so kind to him," she said. "Do you have a family of your own?"

He abruptly froze at her touch and faced her with a guarded look. "I am afraid I have no one, Madam, and I have lingered here far too long."

She removed her hand in an instant, confused by his change in demeanor. She also noticed his warm greeting of "Miss" changed to a decisively cold "Madam."

"I apologize if I have offended you, Sir," Kaitlin spoke, her eyes wide.

The handsome stranger's strong jaw was set hard and unmovable. She instinctively knew she'd seen a gentle side of this man that he most likely never showed the world, and he considered it a weakness.

"I must be on my way," he said evenly, any emotion he may have held gone from his eyes as if he were never capable of such a thing.

With a brief nod she was left at the curb holding her bag and trying to control her trembling heart. His touch on her skin left a strange warmth that didn't dissipate and the sound of his voice filled her thoughts with memories she could almost see on the horizon of her mind as the taxi she numbly got into ferried her into the heart of the city.

•

The hotel was not extravagant because she didn't want to draw attention to herself, but it was nice and clean, and located near the Kahn where a person could buy, sell or trade just about anything in the world.

She checked in with ease and sat on the plush bed with the curtains drawn to try to rest for a moment. Kaitlin loved Cairo—not the side tourists see, but the people and the history. She was passionate about the ancient nooks and secret repositories hidden throughout the city, filled with scholars and scrolls and many things the average traveler never encountered. It had taken her many years to make friends and connections among the scholars and treasure hunters, so distant in their mysterious cliques and societies.

It was just such a friend who sent the medallion to New York. Kaitlin had worked with Nigel on a few assignments in the past, and he was very good at his job, though she wondered why he had specifically asked for her and made mention that no one else was to be sent in her stead were she unable to take the assignment.

A slight shiver ran down her spine at the thought of seeing him again. She'd always found him attractive; his shoulder length, thick brown hair and amber eyes were as enticing as his English accent. During the time they were associated she'd been struggling to save her marriage and Nigel was always a perfect gentleman. She wondered if he'd treat her differently now.

Kaitlin took a deep breath and allowed herself to think of Alex. She'd stayed in the marriage longer than she should have, long enough that his own family let her know they'd understand if she were to try to move on with her life.

"Well, I did try to move on," she muttered under her breath. "And look what happened." She stood and crossed the room to a full length mirror supported by a lovely dark wooden frame and two hinges.

"Let's have a look and see if I'm worth having now," she said to herself and adjusted the glass to reflect her figure.

Her linen pants were wrinkled beyond all hope and she had a thin layer of sparkling dust coating the rest of her clothing. She slipped the clips from her hair and shook it free; it cascaded down her shoulders to the small of her back. She removed her travel-worn outfit and stood in her underclothes, appraising herself.

"Mid-thirties, decent tan ..." She turned to the side and stood up straight, laughing at her reflection. No matter how hard she worked to keep her figure trim, she always felt she could do more.

"Things will seem much better after a nice, hot shower," Kaitlin told her twin in the mirror, who nodded back at her.

It seemed forever until the water in the shower grew warm. She stood on the mat because the tiles were uncommonly cool to the touch. As the room began to steam, she opened the frosted glass door and stepped inside. The water felt luxurious as it slipped over her skin, not just cleansing her body, but rinsing away the stress and weariness of her long flight.

She lathered the sweet scented soap with her fingers, rubbing her aching muscles. She was immediately reminded of her dream, of the strong, slick fingers on her skin. Without realizing, she began to stroke herself in the same manner, her hands grazing her full, rounded breasts.

The water smoothly caressed her body, tingling like a lover's soft kiss and she gasped with surprise at her state of arousal, becoming aware of her surroundings once again. She wasn't sure how long she'd been standing under the spray, but the water was growing cooler in a rapid manner and she quickly dropped her daydream to rinse off the remaining lather.

She stepped from the shower and dried off with the thick, soft towel provided by the hotel.

"Egyptian Cotton," she said out loud, smiling. "Of course."

She noticed a tray, which held a sampling of exotic oils and perfumes in various colored glass bottles and vials on the vanity table. There was a note nestled among the little treasures and she gracefully reached out to take it.

"My dear Kaitlin," she read aloud from the card. "I hope you enjoy this gift. Until we meet, I remain ever your well-wisher. Nigel."

She smiled to herself and put the card down, exchanging it for a deep ruby vial that sparkled in the soft light like a jewel. Gingerly removing the top, she pulled out the long glass stem and grazed her naked wrist with the warm, sensuous oil. She raised her arm and caught the scent of deep, rich sandalwood.

Instantly Kaitlin became dizzy and grabbed the edge of the vanity to steady herself. Her vision grew dark around the edges and she thought she could hear the crackle of a torch in the distance.

As her vision narrowed ever further a face appeared before her, not the shadowy figure from her dream, not even Nigel from whom the gift was sent.

It was the stranger from the airport she beheld and her heart beat faster, leaving her breathless.

The last thing she remembered before she collapsed was the deep blue of his stormy eyes.

•

It was a rhythmic sound. She could almost sleep if it wasn't so insistent. A cool breeze washed over her face in waves and she opened her eyes. She could barely make out the ceiling fan above the bed in her hotel room.

When everything came into focus, she turned her head to see

a kindly, older gentleman with stark white hair sitting on a chair next to her bed smiling.

"There you are, young lady." He reached out and put two fingers on her wrist. "Lie still while I count your pulse, please."

It was impossible to resist such a firm request, so she did as she was asked.

"I'm Doctor David Hollinger," he said when he was finished. "You may call me Doctor David Hollinger."

He grinned and she smiled back, instantly at ease.

"Go ahead and sit up if you like." He gestured toward the extra pillows stacked beside her. When she was upright, he continued. "The maid service found you. I'm afraid you scared the wits out of a rather impressionable young lady."

"I'm truly sorry," Kaitlin began, pressing a hand to her forehead. "Things have been a little difficult for me lately. I've suffered a death in the family." Upon saying this she looked away briefly, but the alert physician noted her deference to the statement. "Now I've taken a new job and haven't had a lot of time to adjust."

"The hotel concierge informed me you flew in from the States just a short while ago. It's likely you are suffering from jet lag, as well as no small amount of stress. I recommend you take it easy for a little while, until you get your bearings and adapt to your new surroundings." He pulled a business card out of his pocket and handed it to her. "My office is just across the street from this hotel. Please feel free to visit me anytime you may need something, or if you would just like to talk."

Kaitlin nodded thankfully and took the card as he stood.

"Remember, young lady—" He turned from the doorway as he was exiting the room. "You've had a lot of changes in your life. No matter how far you might travel the globe, sooner or later you must come to terms with your past, so you can have a future."

"I know that all too well, Doctor," Kaitlin smiled sadly, thinking of Alex. If only …

"We're all given a gift in this lifetime," he told her gently as he pulled the door closed behind him. "Though we may not always be able to control the things that happen to us, we can always control the lessons we learn from them. That's how we build character."

His words struck a chord of truth deep within her spirit and she felt herself becoming stronger as she prepared for the adventure ahead.

•

It was early evening and the streets near the bazaar were becoming crowded as the sun dipped gently behind the horizon and the air cooled.

The stone and sand glowed a deep red from the passing light as Kaitlin easily navigated the back alleyways toward her destination. She was aware of the dangers in the back streets, just as she was aware of the eyes that watched her progression. She kept her swift, confident stride without skipping a beat. Weakness was never a sign to show the denizens of this city.

She came to an unmarked stone archway and slipped through. It was dark in the stairwell leading down, but she knew the steps well and came to the bottom where an iron grate separated her from the rest of the passage.

The medallion was tucked safely inside her jacket pocket, yet it grew so warm she removed her coat and draped it over her left arm. With her free arm she slipped her hand through the grate into the darkness beyond, feeling for the bell she knew to be on the other side.

She rang it three times and waited patiently.

Kaitlin sat on the lower step in front of the grate, her jacket across her knees, feeling the unusual warmth of the relic through all the cloth. Eventually, a soft light appeared in the distance and she heard the sound of sandals shuffling through the narrow stone corridor. As the light approached, she heard a short laugh and a hurried few steps to close the distance.

"Hestor!" she exclaimed, blinking at the weathered brown face in the lamp light.

"Welcome back, Lovely One," he spoke with a thick accent, but Kaitlin understood him perfectly well. "Nigel has told me you might come to pay me a visit."

Hestor had a loud and booming voice, quite the contrast against his tiny stature and ancient visage. He pulled out a large ring holding several brass and silver keys, selecting the one to unlock the door. Once inside the passage, Kaitlin hugged him warmly and bent down to give him a kiss on the cheek.

"Ah, Lovely One," he laughed out loud, blushing even through his sun-darkened skin as they traveled down the length of the corridor. "Have you reconsidered my offer of marriage? Remember, all of this could be yours!"

His arms swept wide through the small room they entered; it was no larger than her hotel room, but far more special. Lining almost every inch of wall space were shelves laden with airtight containers of all different shapes and sizes. She knew inside each was a rare scroll or valuable item. Her friend was quite a collector, as well as a leading expert in Coptic translation.

"I would be honored to consider your proposal one day." Kaitlin grinned at her companion.

"That is what you always say," he replied, waving a hand in mock despair.

They laughed together and he led her to a small table near one corner of the room. This table held an electric light as well as many instruments necessary for his line of work. He pulled out a chair and she sat down with a nod.

"Now," he seated himself across from her, leaning forward almost eagerly, "Nigel has not told me much, and I have been unable to reach him since he contacted me regarding your arrival."

"I think I probably know even less," Kaitlin added, a hopeful look on her face.

"Then I shall tell you what I do know. He was with a pretty standard expedition, the usual Atlantis diving team scenario, searching the underwater caverns off the shore of Alexandria." He paused, aware of Kaitlin's passion for such things, and certainly her eyes became brighter. "From what I understand, they discovered an ancient ship in a submerged cove well under sea level. At one time it must have been above the water, but the ship became trapped inside the cave, preserved in a perfect pocket of air.

"In time, she fell to pieces, but it seems as if everything on board was completely undisturbed. And, they found more than the items that day." His voice dropped to a soft whisper. "A sailor or some such stranger was found in the cove along with the remains of the ship. He is said to have no memory of how he arrived at the location, or even of who he is. But he knows about every item on that find. He is said to be a strong and unyielding man, and he somehow must have persuaded the team to take him on. Truly his knowledge about the items would have been helpful. In time, he was running everything."

"Perhaps he's looking for answers." Kaitlin sighed. "As we all are."

"I suppose you will find out soon." He winked. "Nigel left the expedition almost as soon as they emerged with the first recovery, which leads me to believe he procured his find without permission."

Kaitlin knew the profession well and nodded her agreement.

"He sent it to my publisher not very long after, to get it out of his hands, I'd guess," she added. "I really have no idea how he arranged it, just that a courier dropped it off at the publication. I imagine he's keeping a pretty low profile right now."

"I assume you have it?" He arched an eyebrow with barely

concealed excitement.

"You assume correctly." Her eyes sparkled as she gingerly re-moved the medallion from her pocket and laid the bundle on the table.

"May I?" he inquired, his hands flexing at the ready.

Kaitlin gave him an affirming look and he ceremoniously un-wrapped the package.

Hestor drew a sharp breath as the item was revealed. "Mag-nificent," he exhaled, picking it up. The chain rested in one hand while the great, heavy circle was cradled in the other. "Warm to the touch. How odd," he whispered as if someone else might hear.

"Yes, very curious," she responded. "At times it even feels hot. I don't understand what causes it."

He appeared enraptured by the item, his fingers stroking the intricate chain. Kaitlin watched him carefully as his breathing became shallow and a rapt expression settled onto his face. She wondered if she'd had that same look in the taxi in front of the airport.

"Hestor," she spoke softly at first, but got no response. "Can you hear me?"

"Yes, my princess. I await your word."

Kaitlin offered him a quizzical stare after being addressed in such a manner, but he often used endearments with her. She roughly grabbed his arm and shook him. Her concern deepened as he attempted to raise the chain over his head. He seemed to snap out of a heavy daze, a bit confused and disoriented as he re-garded her with wide eyes. He abruptly sat the relic on the table.

"Well?" she inquired, trying not to be impatient.

"I—" he began, his voice a bit shaky but filled with wonder as he gazed at her. "I cannot say."

With a visible effort, he turned his attention back to the medal-lion. She noticed at this point that he didn't touch it again, but used tools to move it and hold it under different lights and magnifying glasses.

"Yes, yes," he noted to himself as he studied the surface. "Look here, Kaitlin."

She approached his side of the table and bent over his shoulder. Though there appeared to be many symbols, looking through the glass, there was one significant symbol over all. No matter how one viewed each section, everything formed into that shape.

"Let's see." Hestor jumped up rather spryly from his chair and went to part of the wall that held a glass-enclosed bookcase.

Carefully, he removed a very old tome, its thick leather cover worn and cracked with time. With great patience he slowly opened the book and seemed to know which page he was searching for.

"There." He pointed and Kaitlin leaned in to see. Though she didn't understand the script surrounding the symbol, she could plainly see a six-pointed star.

"This is often referred to as the Seal of Solomon," he began, tracing it with his fingers. "The upright triangle represents the fiery male while the inverted triangle represents the watery female. If you look closely at Nigel's find, you will see that all the inscriptions form an upright triangle, from the smallest symbol to the entire engraving."

"The fiery male," Kaitlin repeated to herself, her curiosity about the item growing. She noticed once more that he didn't touch the medallion with his skin as he wrapped it up and handed it to her.

"That would be all I could tell you without further study, Lovely One, except this—" He paused to make sure he had her full attention. "Nigel, while a charming man, most often does nothing that will not benefit himself in some way. He asked to see you personally. Be wary of his intentions."

"Thank you, Hestor," she said with great sincerity. "You hold a special place in my heart."

"Yes, yes," he said all over again. "That is what you always say. Just remember my offer!"

Chapter Two

It was fully dark as she made her way back to the hotel. Nighttime in this city had a special quality, as if it wrapped itself in a luxurious velvet drape, nestling in among the crevices and doorways, blanketing its secrets with enticing mystery and darkness.

She reached the hotel without incident, her hand tucked into her pocket and resting on the package she was beginning to hold dear.

She swept in off the streets into the lobby and went directly to the front desk in anticipation. The attendant smiled at her a little too eagerly and Kaitlin wondered if she'd just missed something.

"Are there any messages for Kaitlin Sommers?" she inquired a little impatiently.

"Just one, Miss," he replied, suppressing a laugh. She began to become a little nervous.

"Well, may I have it?"

"Certainly," a deep, cultured English voice spoke from the lobby behind her. "If you would be so kind as to turn around?"

For an eternity it seemed, her heart failed to beat and she had trouble breathing. As she turned through the thick web that slowed her motions, ages must have passed.

Nigel was amazingly handsome. Standing over six feet tall, his deep brown hair was streaked with gold, accenting his glowing amber eyes. He smiled in such a way that she felt weak. A pristine white shirt graced his lean and muscular frame. He stood easily in the lobby, holding a bouquet of flowers.

"I had these flown in from Paris for you, just this afternoon."

He approached her with an enchanting smile. Kaitlin was overwhelmed and blushing much too furiously to reply.

"It is indeed a pleasure to see your lovely face once more, my dear."

He took her hand and bent gently over it, raising his eyes to hers as his lips grazed the sensitive skin on the back of her fingers. She felt his warm breath, the slight moisture, as he casually let one sigh fall upon her hand. She stood with her jaw slightly open in a rather unladylike manner.

"Wow," the clerk whispered, staring at the couple.

"My good man," Nigel flourished a rather large American bill into the air. "Would you kindly locate a vase to accompany my gift to the lady and have it delivered to her room at your convenience?"

"Of course, Sir," the clerk said again, nearly tripping over his own two feet to get to the bouquet. When he was gone, Nigel turned his full attention to Kaitlin once again.

"I was hoping you would come along with me to dinner this evening? I would be honored to have you by my side to discuss business."

Kaitlin must have frowned at the mention of business because he added "among other things" with a rather appreciative look.

"Could I take a few moments to get ready?" she asked hopefully, looking at her blue jeans and sandals.

"Anything you need."

"Anything?" she repeated breathlessly, the blush returning to her cheeks once again.

"I shall await you in the lobby, then?" He urged her forward with a firm hand and patient look.

Kaitlin was extremely aware that his eyes watched her as she desperately attempted to stroll nonchalantly to the elevator. Putting one foot in front of the other at that moment was one of the most difficult feats of grace she'd ever managed to accomplish. Once inside her room, however, it was a different story and chaos reigned as she stumbled over shoes and tossed unworthy dresses over her shoulder.

"Why did I ever pack this?" she almost wailed in despair, letting a rather frumpy, eggplant colored blouse fall to the floor.

"Simple is best. Keep it simple," she murmured to herself, releasing a long, black silk dress from the garment bag she'd been assaulting.

She removed her street clothes and pulled on a pair of black satin panties. As quickly as she could, she slid a matching pair of black stockings up her long legs to rest at the middle of her thighs.

The dress lay on the bed and she realized it was not made to be worn with much in the way of a bra, so she held her breath and let it fall over her head and settle on her shapely figure. The silk was impossibly soft, the thin shoulder straps holding the delicate fabric up just enough to drape over her full breasts. It hung low in the back, lower than anything she'd ever worn before and she hoped the fact that the gown touched her toes would make up for the exposure she felt on top.

"There's no turning back now," Kaitlin said to her twin in the glass. This time she looked like a beautiful stranger as she let her hair loose to fall where it had a mind to as she watched. Stepping into her black leather heels, she walked briefly into the bathroom to apply a deep red gloss to her nervous lips.

"It's only business," she said to herself. "Nothing to get worked up over." But she knew it had been a long time since she felt anything romantic in her life, long before Alex's death—and her senses seemed to be awakening at all the wrong times.

She paused momentarily at the tray of exotic oils and pulled the red vial free. With a quick movement, she drew the stem from the bottle and slid it slowly between her breasts. The same feeling came over her that she'd had when she originally experienced the scent, only this time she thought she heard a voice.

"You are mine—forever," it whispered.

Kaitlin swayed momentarily and shook her head to clear it.

"I must be losing my mind," she muttered under her breath as she left the bathroom and grabbed her bag. A white business card fell from the night stand and fluttered to the floor as she passed.

"Doctor Hollinger," she said conversationally in the empty room. "I think I may pay you a visit after all."

The elevator door opened and she walked nervously into the lobby. Nigel saw her first and there was no mistaking the look of awe in his eyes. He stood perfectly still for a moment as she continued forward, then came to life as if he just remembered where he was and what he was doing.

"I must say, you look stunning," he said sincerely and offered her his arm. She placed her left hand in the crook of his elbow and he intimately covered it with his own.

As they walked toward the lobby where the attendant waited to open the door, he carefully stroked the fingers she'd placed in his possession. When he felt no wedding ring there, he glanced at her questioningly, but said nothing.

"Wow," the clerk said as he opened the door and released them into the night.

•

The linens on the table were a pure white, glowing in the candlelight that made up the only illumination in the room. They were alone in the small space, a very extravagant move on her charming companion's part.

Her head spun from the heavy smell of spices, so rich and decadent with flavor coming from the main dining area. Kaitlin almost felt as if she were waking from a dream where she had slept far too long, and everything around her seemed to arouse such extreme responses.

She hadn't realized how long it had been since she'd had a decent meal, and as Nigel held the chair out for her to sit at their elegant table, she thought many of her needs had been neglected for longer than she cared to remember.

Nigel didn't sit opposite her, but stood nearby, regarding her in a rather pensive manner.

"May I pour you a glass of red wine, Kaitlin?"

The way he spoke her name was almost sensual, so intimate in its familiarity. She shivered slightly, but nodded as he crossed the small space to an ice bucket holding a bottle opened and ready. With perfect motion he poured a small amount in each glass, the deep ruby liquid sparkling within the crystal goblets. The fragrance was overwhelmingly heady from a distance. He approached her carefully and still seemed as if he were considering something.

"I always remembered your beautiful eyes, you know," he said as he moved closer with her glass. "I couldn't have imagined you would grow lovelier since we last met, and yet, it has happened and your breathless beauty has captured me."

Kaitlin reached out to take the goblet he offered and as her fingers closed around the stem, he slid his hand down to cover hers gently. With the lightest urge, he tipped the glass toward her mouth and she sipped delicately at the red wine he had chosen.

The knock on the door to their private room was so unobtrusive that she barely noticed. Nigel did, however, and instantly regained his composure. She wondered how he could do that so easily while she remained at the table in a quivering heap as the server brought in their food.

The table was laden with more exotic dishes than she could have imagined in one place, and she thought briefly of the small child at the airport. How much food could he buy for his family from the cost of this one meal?

The thought of the unfortunate boy brought back an uninvited recollection of the stranger at the airport and she shook her head slightly to clear her vision of his deep, troubled eyes. She was instantly brought back to the proper place and time as Nigel took his seat across from her, a serious look on his face. It almost felt like the lull just before a play when the stage was being set.

"We need to discuss a few things before I send you into the lion's den, so to speak." He frowned slightly and she felt a great deal of disappointment at the change of subject inspired by the interruption.

Pulling together her composure, she nodded confidently and he smiled his approval.

"As you may have already guessed, the item I placed temporarily in your possession was procured by rather illegitimate means and I'm afraid the expedition leader wouldn't be a bit fond of me at the moment. I have someone on the inside, of course, to get you in. But once he puts you in contact with this despicable character, this stranger who cut into all our livelihoods by taking over, you'll be on your own."

"What do you mean exactly?" Kaitlin was more disturbed by the mention of her "temporary possession" than by his reference to her danger.

"They call him Sol—if that's even his name. He moved the entire find by means we know nothing about because we can't trace it, and only allows a very precious few access to the items. My contact has arranged for you to be one of those few. You have a skill and talent we don't. You have your art."

At this he looked away and added quietly, "Not to mention a considerable beauty."

"So—" She felt she needed her glass refilled after that statement. "Once I'm placed in this questionable man's care, I'll be taken to a location unknown to any of you."

Nigel nodded, watching her carefully. If he thought she was worried about her own safety, he was wrong. She had many other things on her mind, mostly his motives for using her to do this assignment.

"You want to know where he relocated the find," she stated flatly as he moved to a different bottle of wine.

"I'm trying to protect the interests of everyone involved, my dear," he said smoothly, his voice taking on a well-rehearsed tone.

"And what of my interests?" She smiled straightforwardly.

He laughed a little, caught off guard. "May I interest you in a lovely, crisp white wine?"

"I suppose that will have to do for a start." She sighed dramatically and picked up a second glass for the new spirit.

The room had grown rather warm, the candles in the small space affecting the temperature. Kaitlin thought she could see a hint of moonlight through the gauzy curtains hiding the double doors next to the table, and rose abruptly to part them. They were heavier than they looked and she struggled with them for a few moments.

"If you make it through and there's snow and a faun on the other side, you'll have to come right back and let me know." Nigel chuckled from the table where he was being absolutely no help at all.

She made it past the yards of fabric and opened the doors onto a small balcony a few stories above the street. The air was still warm but dry, and a gentle breeze blew through the complicated maze of streets and alleys. The moon was full and cast a remarkable silver gloss on her skin and hair. She felt bathed in the soft, gentle light, as if her soul were being cleansed of its recent heaviness.

"Moonlight becomes you," he said almost breathlessly as he joined her outside.

Kaitlin smiled because he sounded so sincere, and leaned against the railing, face upturned and basking in the ethereal light that stirred such primal passions within.

Nigel stood close behind her not quite touching the exposed

back she'd innocently turned to him. Slowly, as if filled with purpose, he reached out two furtive hands that almost slipped onto her shoulders unnoticed. With a sigh, he pressed his hold more firmly on her skin and stood her upright.

"We can't have you taking a fall over the side now, can we?" he asked her in an admonishing tone.

It was then she saw the shadow below. It was darker than the rest of the alley and shaped like a man. If she focused, she thought maybe he was watching them, moving ever so slightly, and her expert ears picked up the sound of an almost silent shutter clicking away.

Nigel immediately felt her change, felt her interest draw away and he peered in the direction she was staring. As soon as he made out the size and shape, the shadow sprang to life and sprinted down the alley.

Nigel gave a shout and a moment later their small room was filled with concerned restaurant staff. She knew there was no possible way to catch or identify the uninvited voyeur, but once Nigel settled the staff, there was no doubt the mood was broken.

Kaitlin was disappointed by the remainder of the meal because her companion seemed very rushed and agitated. Undoubtedly the stranger in the shadows had photographed them, but why? The walk back to her hotel was strained to say the least, and she knew Nigel was at the limit of his accommodating nature by pushing her so quickly to end the evening.

"Is there anything else I should know before I rendezvous with your man at the appointed time?" she asked as he escorted her quickly into the lobby, knowing he wouldn't answer her in any case.

"It may be best if no one knows why you're here, my dear," he whispered in her ear as he left her at the elevator. Without a moment's hesitation, he turned from her and exited the hotel, offering no further explanation.

Chapter Three

Her room was totally dark. Thick, dark blinds lined the window space behind the curtains to keep out the light, and likely a large amount of heat as well. She thought she was awake, but didn't wish to roll over and look at the clock. Her head ached slightly and she remembered how much wine she'd consumed the night before over the strained and hurried dinner.

"My first date in years," she mumbled to herself, face buried in one of the plush pillows that decorated her bed. "A disaster, of course."

She burrowed deeper under the covers and started to drift off to sleep again when her phone began to ring. After a few brief minutes of blindly feeling along the bedside table, she grasped the receiver and pulled it off its cradle. Though the phone lay against her pillow just a few short inches from her ear, she could clearly hear the bright and cheery voice on the other end.

"Good morning, Lovely One!" Hestor practically beamed through the phone, if such a thing were possible. Kaitlin instinctively shut her eyes.

"Oh, Hestor," she groaned, moving the phone away another inch or two. "Is it morning already?"

"You know what they say. The early bird gets the worm," he responded warmly.

"Maybe so. But the worm gets eaten," she protested, and felt for the lamp near the phone.

"I have some more information on your interesting artifact," he teased, knowing that would get her up and about. "Would you care to join me for breakfast and a fantastic tale of love and tragedy born in the heart of Persia?"

"Since you put it like that, I can hardly see how I might resist." She smiled over the phone, unable to carry on a grumpy attitude faced with such engaging conversation.

"Good! Then meet me at our spot in an hour. I will be waiting with admirable patience until I can see your lovely face once again." He laughed and ended the call.

•

Kaitlin often had breakfast with Hestor when she was visiting the city, and luckily their favorite spot was very close to the Kahn. She was even early as she arrived, but not before Hestor. He rose from his chair as she approached, an endless smile of pleasure on his face upon seeing her.

He moved around the small table and helped her into her seat. A large ceramic carafe sat to one side of the table and she could imagine the thick, hearty taste of the coffee he preferred. The morning air was already hot and oppressive, but she found a cup of coffee was about the only thing she wanted in the world at that moment. As if reading her thoughts, Hestor took the initiative and poured her a cup, just the way she liked it.

He sat back, regarding her as she sipped the brew, the flavor sending new life through her veins. He seemed about to burst with news of the artifact.

"So," she began in a playful voice, "you say you've found additional information on the medallion, and you're in love with someone from Persia?"

He laughed out loud in a manner that drew some attention to their table, then leaned forward slightly.

"Only with you, Lovely One. There can be no one else for me."

"Do tell," she encouraged, her interest aroused by his excitement.

"What do you know of the Djinn?" Hestor asked, his face masked in intrigue.

"Do you mean a Genie? Like Aladdin?" she answered a little confused.

"Actually, Aladdin had the lamp that the Djinn came from, but yes, that is what I mean. Hollywood has shaped what we know of the Djinn into a rather friendly, helpful being. That is not always what they were in legend."

"What were they? And what does that have to do with the medallion?"

"The legends say they are mischievous tricksters, born of fire, and rank just below angels or devils in the scheme of things. They are well known for interfering with the course of human nature as they see fit, for amusement or personal gain. Some say they grant wishes and others say they twist your desires in such a way that nothing you wish for will happen in the way you imagined."

"I did hear something like that. I've come across pieces of research from time to time about it, but never really considered the legend too deeply." Kaitlin thought about the medallion and the symbol that occurred repeatedly across its surface. "The fiery male!" she exclaimed, making the connection.

Hestor smiled like a teacher who had finally gotten through to his favorite pupil. He reached under the table and pulled up a leather satchel, removing a scroll and setting it on the table between them.

"It is just a copy, of course," he explained as she looked at it in surprise. "It is still ancient in its own right, but I traced the story inscribed on this scroll to a collection of tales that supposedly was kept in the original Library of Alexandria before it was destroyed."

"Where did you find this?" She was astonished by his resourcefulness.

"Let's just say a network of associates in the kind of business we are in hunger for only two things," he said. "The first is, of course, knowledge. The second is the ability to show one another up with our infinite wisdom and ownership of the items we deal in. A colleague of mine was more than happy to help me with the information I was lacking and generously allow me to use this rare but not priceless copy."

Hestor chuckled as he opened the scroll and held it flat in the middle of the table. The scroll was also in a script Kaitlin was unfamiliar with, but she instantly recognized a faded sketch of the medallion. It was almost identical to hers, though it looked as if perhaps some symbols here and there may have gotten lost over the years. Still, it was an elaborate work of art in and of itself and there was no denying the fact that it was her medallion. She laughed a little at that thought, that she considered it hers.

"I will translate this text for you if you like, though it will take a while. Until then, would you like to hear the premise of the story?" He smiled, knowing the answer.

"Yes, please," she said quickly, unable to keep her fingers from tapping on the table.

"This will just be an outline, really, until I can work on it further, but here is what I can tell you now. It seems to take place a long, long time ago, possibly during the time when Macedonia was still considered a barbarian land, before Alexander the Great was even born."

Kaitlin nodded and wondered if there was any possibility the medallion could be that old. Surely it must be a copy from another made during that time.

"This is a tale of tragedy and lost love. It seems there were many nations in Persia, all warring with one another with their sights to the west and the land they all hungered for there. But there was one man who was different—a prince of a nation whose name was lost by the time of the writing.

"This prince had fallen in love with a mere temple slave, one with a beauty and innocence so great that the mere sight of her could either instigate a war or end all siege." He paused and looked closely at the scroll.

"This is where the translation gets a little fuzzy. It says this is their story and it clearly states that against all tradition, he took the initiative to make her his wife. From what I can understand, his father and the advisors of the kingdom did not favor this union, and in truth, his father was ill and the Prince was to be groomed to replace him in the great land war of the West. Of course the Prince had no desire to fight and die, to ever leave the side of his one true love.

"Apparently, in a devious plot of treachery, a murder was attempted by someone with an interest in the future of the kingdom and the land to be had by the new strategy of the war. I think they are telling us the Prince found her poisoned, near her death, and no one in the kingdom was able to cure her.

"Her assassination was long, cruel and torturous. It was a deliberate attempt to harden the Prince's heart and turn aside all love from him forever. His guilt grew after days of watching her suffer, knowing he should ease her pain and end it, but not being able to let go. That was probably what drew the stranger to his side; people like that always sense desperation.

"He came in the night, his cloak as dark as the new moon and the air around him as cold as the tomb. This stranger made him an offer he could not refuse. If he could retrieve a family heirloom belonging to the mysterious man, he could save the life of the Prince's most beloved."

Kaitlin realized she was holding her breath as he paused again in an attempt to make out more of the writing.

"I must skip this part for now. I cannot decipher it. Let me continue near the end," he said in disappointment.

"The heirloom he wanted was a medallion, and only a prince of noble blood could retrieve it from the depths of the lair in which it was hidden. The Prince did as he was told, and we come to the end here.

"It says the stranger becomes greedy, and attempts to wrest the item from the Prince before he can hand it over. It was that greed that did him in, for the Prince would have gladly given him the medallion on sight. The stranger crept into the Prince's chambers as he slept bone-weary after the battle to get the artifact, and tried to steal it. He was caught by a personal guard who always remained unnoticed in the royal chambers at all times.

"A terrible fight ensued and the stranger was run through with a pair of wicked scimitars. On his deathbed he gazed into the Prince's eyes and saw that they held true love for his bride so he told him the secret of the medallion: it would grant him one wish but at a terrible price—to cast the wish he must chain the medallion upon his neck, never to be removed again. He would get his wish, but he would be bound by immortality as Djinn for all eternity and forced to live outside the world of mortals.

"For the Prince, it was a small price to pay—his life for that of his bride. Without a moment of hesitation, he put the medallion around his neck. It seared with the flame of untold ages, a magic deeper than any we have come to understand in all our wisdom. He was bound. He was cast out.

"He went immediately to her chamber, only to find it empty. He could still smell the lingering scent of the herbs they burned to cover the smell of sickness that could permeate every particle of a deathbed room. The Prince ran down the corridors like a mad man, his mind slipping away. Finally, he reached the set of rooms belonging to the healers they employed. There was much weeping and sadness coming from inside and a chill filled his heart like an eclipse on his soul.

"'Where is she?' He cried long tears of fear and loss. They shook their heads. They could not answer. He left them in their sorrow and found the stairwell that wound deep into the passages underneath the palace. The air was cool below the earth, but he shivered from more than the change in temperature. He melded with the shadows outside of the embalming chamber, and his hands gripped the medallion so tightly it cut his skin, warm blood coating the surface of the hot metal.

"He knew if the process were complete he could not wish her spirit back into her body and everything he had done to save her was in vain. He found her within, being prepared for burial. The servants were anointing her skin with scented oils, mumbling prayers and wards against the evil spirits that would surely gather around this child for the deed against her.

"The Prince uttered a tortured moan as he saw her there, removed his scimitars from their sheaths, still stained by the blood of the stranger, and in his grief he cut the servants down until their cries were silent. His weapons dropped to the ground and he approached her slowly. The torches on the wall crackled in a fit of anger at the disruption in the air.

"She lay in all her innocent beauty inside her sarcophagus as if she were merely sleeping. Nestled within were the ornate clay jars that held the remains of her wisdom, her love and her life. In a daze, the Prince reached forward and finished the job of the ones he had slain, finished lathering her with the oils, though he could not bear to wrap her skin in the cloth that lay nearby. He brushed her full lips, still warm from the heated essences, with his fingers and in a sudden move of desperation, claimed her mouth in a kiss.

"'You are mine—forever,' he said, pulling away from her, his back against the torchlight as a tear slide down his face. He then covered her with the heavy stone casing, at the same time sheathing his heart in the bitterness of an eternity without her. From that day forward, he was never seen again, but whenever misfortune befell the rule of the kingdom, people often whispered it was the Djinn Prince visiting his sorrow on those who took his love."

Kaitlin stood abruptly, shock numbing her face. She bumped the table and the coffee spilled all over her bag and their food.

Hestor ignored the scroll and rushed to her side to catch her as she slowly spiraled to the ground.

●

"It's not as if I don't enjoy such lovely company, Miss Sommers," Doctor Hollinger gently scolded her as she lay on the examining table in his office.

"I really don't think this dress does a lot for my figure." She grinned, lifting the hem of the generic white hospital gown and inspecting it.

"You'll be the height of fashion in the sick ward at the clinic if you don't slow down, I assure you. Before you try to avoid the subject, would you care to tell me about the kinds of pressures you're dealing with right now? You don't seem to have any unusual infections. Your white blood cell count is normal and aside from a touch of elevated heart rate, you apparently suffer from a small case of stubborn personality." He crossed his arms and waited patiently for her response.

"It's all these marriage proposals, Doctor." She sighed with exaggeration, fanning herself lightly with her hand. "I'm practically irresistible in a subconscious type of way."

"Indeed, I have heard as much from your friend in the waiting area." He frowned. "If you don't intend to share your secrets with me today, we'll have to move you along so I can keep my appointment with the next person I probably won't be of any benefit to." He pointed to her clothes, folded neatly on a rich mahogany chair in the corner. "Please see the receptionist on your way out. I believe your friend has already taken care of the details, but she has a small vial of relaxants and I'd like you to consider taking one the next time you come under stress. That way we don't have to pick you up off the floor anymore."

Kaitlin slid gently off the soft leather padding on the examination table and crossed the room to give the doctor a hug.

"Now, that's quite alright," he said gruffly, patting her on the back. He took her by the shoulders and held her out at arms length. "If you do receive any more proposals, you let them know they must be interviewed by me first, young lady."

"I certainly will, Doctor Hollinger." Kaitlin smiled to herself as he left the room.

The late morning sun invaded the comfortable office, slanting through the shades and giving the rich wood furniture a warm, earthy glow. She felt as if she had just awakened from a deep dream that had lasted for a lifetime, and although she was a little confused about the memories the story had stirred within her, she felt perfectly fine otherwise.

Somewhere deep inside was a sense of longing, a passionate need she couldn't translate into her own feelings just then. She dressed slowly, enjoying this quiet time. It wouldn't be much longer before she was sent to a strange place filled with others she didn't know. She shivered with excitement and apprehension.

Hestor's voice rang out in laughter as she walked down the corridor to the reception room. He turned immediately and held out his arms as she entered. She went to him and laid her head on his chest like a small child.

"I hear you are going to be just fine, Lovely One," he said with great affection in his voice. Kaitlin pulled back and looked into his face apologetically.

"I'm so sorry you had to wait for me, Hestor. And I'm terribly sorry about the scroll. I hope I didn't ruin it for you."

"Of course not!" he exclaimed. "It was completely undamaged and even if it were not, it is a small price against someone as valuable as you. And I had fine company while waiting. This gentleman was kind enough to set aside his time so that the doctor could see you immediately."

Kaitlin turned slowly, the hair on the back of her neck standing up as waves of electricity swept through her body. Before she saw him fully, she caught the scent of sandalwood lingering in the lobby.

The stranger from the airport rose from his seat, a look of surprise on his handsome face.

"We must stop meeting in such ways." His soft, melodic voice addressed her.

Kaitlin gazed into his deep blue eyes, afraid to breathe, afraid he would disappear.

"Kaitlin, you know this fellow? What have you been up to, then?" Hestor chuckled, not noticing the effect the stranger had on her.

The man slowly approached and stood before her, his hands trembling slightly as he reached out and brushed the hair from Kaitlin's eyes.

"We met briefly at the airport when she arrived in Cairo," he answered Hestor simply as he returned his gaze to Kaitlin. "I hope you are well. Your friend has been greatly concerned for you."

Words didn't seem to have a place in front of this stranger, and in any case, Kaitlin couldn't think of anything to say. Her senses were overwhelmed with thoughts and dreams of the slightest touch of his hand on her forehead. Though she was standing a normal distance from him, she could feel herself pressed against his strong chest, his arms holding her tight and the taste of his lips against hers, exotic and sweet.

The receptionist coughed politely and Kaitlin became aware the woman was standing quite near holding the medicine Doctor Hollinger had offered.

"He's ready for you." She nodded to the stranger. He gazed into Kaitlin's eyes one last time, a mixture of desire and confusion on his face as he turned and abruptly exited the waiting area.

Wordlessly, Kaitlin plucked the bottle from the receptionist's hand and opened it, immediately removing two capsules and swallowing them.

"You really have quite an effect on people," Hestor said as he ushered her across the crowded street to the hotel.

"I kind of thought it was the other way around," she murmured softly as her friend took the list of things she needed for her journey out of her hand.

Once inside her suite, Hestor rang for the cart and ordered tea.

"I will head into the market and fill your list while you rest easy for a while." He smiled and gave her a brief hug.

"You don't have to run my errands, Hestor. I can get the things I need before I leave."

"And you don't have to leave, if you do not wish it," he responded with a slightly reprimanding tone. "Remember what I said about Nigel. I have no reason to believe he would endanger you, but he is definitely up to something and I don't care a lot for that."

"Thank you for your concern," she said. "But Hestor, I need to know more about the medallion. I can't let this go. I know it's important and I have to find out why. I don't know how else to explain it."

"I understand. Believe me, I do. We share a lot of the same passions, you know." He reflected inwardly for a moment and the same look of wonder that he'd held the day he touched the amulet passed across his face. "But I feel this is your journey, not mine. I hope the doors to your soul open along the way and you find the wings you need to fly."

Kaitlin grew pensive as she reflected on the strange wording he used before he left her alone in her room. Her tea arrived just minutes after he'd gone and her clothes were already dusty after such a short time in the city. After rifling through the wardrobe for a moment she pulled on a soft, satin dressing gown.

She sighed and laid down on the freshly made bed. It wasn't long before she drifted into the early stages of sleep where the slightest sound or touch is amplified a thousand times. She heard footsteps cross the tiles in front of her door and become muted by the carpet, but her head was so heavy she couldn't lift it. She tried to open her eyes to no avail.

Well, maybe two pills out of that bottle was too many, she thought to herself, and imagined it was Hestor returning with the items.

Hestor knew she'd taken something to help relax and would likely let her sleep it off. As she drifted further into the realm of dreams, she didn't notice the weight pulling on the mattress as someone sat beside her.

In her clouded state, she thought she was back in Doctor Hollinger's office. She couldn't remember leaving there that afternoon and realized she must be waiting for him to examine her so she could go. The office was so warm and comfortable; it was easy to fall asleep on the table as she waited.

It felt like a very long time, but eventually someone entered the room. She opened her eyes slightly, but Dr. Hollinger wasn't the newcomer. Her handsome stranger stood with his back to the door, regarding her with expressive eyes.

"I'm sorry," he said immediately, beginning to reach behind himself for the door handle. "I didn't know anyone was in here still. I'll wait outside."

"No," she managed to get out, though her tongue felt heavy and her head could barely move. "Please, don't go."

He approached her apprehensively and she could see the fear in his passionate eyes, his desire for her. With a delicate, almost reverent motion, he took her hand in his. She had little control over her movement, but brought his hand to rest against the outside of her thigh.

The moment his touch grazed her delicate skin, goose bumps spread over her entire body in waves and a small moan of pleasure came from her lips before she could stop it. His breathing increased and it seemed almost against his better judgment that he began to stroke her silky flesh. Her body responded as her back arched and lips parted.

"Touch me with your lips," she begged, helpless at his caress, needing his mouth on her in any way so that she could feel his breath.

"I can deny nothing you ask of me, and that torments me every moment of every day," he whispered as his face came close to hers.

His lips trembled slightly, and whether it was from restraint or worry, she couldn't tell. Suddenly all thought was driven from her mind as his hot mouth covered hers with such strength and need that she could no longer breathe.

When the darkness threatened to engulf her, he pulled away and she felt like the arctic chill of a glacier had covered her skin at his absence. Shamelessly she pressed against him, her gown nearly falling from her frame, and with a heavy sigh of resignation, he brought his mouth against her full breasts, swollen with desire. She gasped at the depths of pleasure she had only dreamed of in the past. She knew this was right. She knew this was where her heart was always meant to be.

"I love you—always," she whispered.

In that instant everything ceased—his touch, his desire and he himself faded away from her. Unable to move, she eventually fell into a deep sleep. She didn't remember she was in her room. She wouldn't remember any of it more than a dream. She didn't see the look on Nigel's face when she told him she loved him. The only evidence that he had even been there was in a sealed envelope on her bedside table.

Kaitlin was awakened by a knock on her door. The sound faded in gradually and she wondered how long it had been going on. She sat up in bed with a woozy feeling and pulled the comforter around her barely dressed figure.

"Come in?" she answered the patient inquiry.

Hestor entered the room, his arms laden with packages and bags.

"I am sorry to be gone so long," he said, setting everything on a nearby table. "I had to go across town for a few things like your magic bottles of elixir."

Kaitlin laughed. He always called the developer and other liquids she used for her film "magic potions."

"Weren't you here a little while ago?" she asked, trying to remember what happened earlier.

"I have been gone all afternoon. First time back thus far. Why do you ask?"

"I just thought someone had come in while I was sleeping. Maybe to drop something off. I assumed it was you." She yawned and stretched a little.

He looked around the room. "Well, the tea cart is still here so none of the staff have come. Or perhaps they did." He hesitated, noticing the envelope next to her bed.

"Was that there before I left?"

"I don't believe so," she answered and reached out to take it. "This is Nigel's writing on the front."

"The concierge must have brought it in, though it is strange for them to come in your room that way when you are sleeping." Hestor mused, scratching his chin.

"Well," Kaitlin figured, "he probably didn't want to leave it at the front desk for anyone to see, so I imagine he sent someone into my room with it so he could be sure I had it."

"That could be the reason." He frowned, but motioned for her to open it.

She read the note silently and then regarded her friend with a nervous look. "This says I leave tonight. I meet his contact at the café where we had breakfast, actually, and go from there."

"I will go with you. Surely Nigel could have no issue with that. Besides, someone has to watch you leave and he doesn't seem to be around a lot lately."

"No, he doesn't," Kaitlin said sourly, but turned a smiling face to Hestor. "You're a very good friend. I don't know what I would do without you."

"I can't imagine the depths of trouble you would fling yourself into at my absence." He laughed. "Having said that, what time shall I return to escort you to the café?"

"This is terribly exciting. You'll like this," she said, raising an eyebrow. "I meet him at sunset."

"I am fretfully jealous, Lovely One," he lamented in an exaggerated manner. "But I will return well before that time to assist you."

"You may regret that offer. My camera equipment is heavy," Kaitlin teased as he left her to her packing.

When he was gone, she pulled items from the bags he left on the table, mentally checking them off the list as she went along. At the bottom of a box of food items, she retrieved a rather expensive bottle of Merlot; it was one of her favorites.

"Hestor, you always think of the important things," she said aloud. "I'll definitely save this for a special occasion."

•

Twilight drove away the last of the colors in the sun-painted sky, and the air around the market held that rare quality one sees just as day gives way to night and casts everything in a surreal clarity.

They chose a table set against the fine sandstone wall that made up so many of the structures in the city. She wanted a place for her equipment to stack up and didn't want anyone coming up behind them.

The streets were narrow and filled with people and carts, selling whatever they had as loudly as possible. The café was on a corner in a bustling area but the dark sedan that pulled up drew attention in the midst of all the noise and chaos regardless.

A tall man emerged from the front passenger side, dressed almost formally with reflective sunglasses on his face. Kaitlin immediately disliked the fact that she couldn't see his eyes as he approached. Hestor stood and greeted him stiffly when he arrived at their table.

"You must be Hestor," the man stated dryly as if he expected to find him here with his charge.

"I am." The tiny man drew himself up as high as possible next to the imposing figure.

"Miss Kaitlin." He nodded in her direction and then snapped

his fingers. The driver exited the black car and made his way over to him. Kaitlin briefly wondered how they found a chauffeur suit in a size that fit this man, and noticed his huge muscular frame straining against the fabric as he began to lift her luggage. Even her largest suitcase looked tiny held up against his barrel-like chest.

"Wait a minute!" she exclaimed as he flung a small briefcase on top of the stack he'd been lifting. "There's sensitive equipment inside and I doubt your employer would be too happy if you broke any of it and made it impossible for me to do my job."

The hulking fellow turned to face her and walked a few steps closer to peer down at her.

"And they said the mountain wouldn't come to Muhammad," Hestor whispered in her ear.

She tried not to smile at his remark and her eyes widened as the driver dropped all her pieces of luggage at her feet and singly carried the briefcase to the car.

"Making friends already, I see," Hestor commented when the man was out of earshot.

"I am afraid we must be going," the tall passenger urged, lightly touching the small of Kaitlin's back to propel her in the direction of the car.

She shrugged off his hand and bent down to pick up her luggage. Hestor grabbed the rest and they set it all inside the trunk, which the helpful driver had left open for them.

She watched the stranger closely out of the corner of her eye as he walked to the front of the vehicle and leaned forward slightly to say something to the driver. He was almost handsome. His skin was a flawless olive tone and his black hair thick and curly. No matter how she tried to perceive him, though, he left her with a slightly oily feeling inside. She hoped he'd never attempt to touch her again and was relieved when he held the car door for her yet kept his distance.

She slipped inside, but as Hestor attempted to gain access as well, he was denied.

"This is as far as you can go," her guide informed Hestor.

He knew better than to argue but his face held a concerned look nonetheless.

"If it makes you feel any better, I am scheduled to meet Nigel here at this same time once a week to accept packages for this young lady's supplies. I am sure you will receive news of her progress then."

"Fair enough," Hestor agreed without much of a choice. Even knowing a little bit helped ease his worry and he planned to meet with Nigel as soon as possible.

•

The ride was filled with an uncomfortable silence. Her new companion elected to travel in the back part of the car with her, yet he seemed decidedly disinclined to chat.

"Hi," Kaitlin stated simply, looking sideways at him.

He merely nodded at her and then resumed his dedicated study of the road ahead.

"I'm Kaitlin," she stated again.

He turned to face her fully this time, the corners of his mouth turned down. "Yes, I am aware of that."

"I noticed. This is the part where you'd usually tell me your name." She crossed her arms and returned his stare.

"I am called Panos. We do not need to be friends. I am here to fulfill my end of an agreement with your associate, Nigel, in return for something you needn't concern yourself with."

"Fine." She nodded at him in agreement. "You aren't my type anyway." His scowl deepened and she suppressed a grin. "I don't suppose you can tell me where we're going?"

"We will arrive at the airport shortly," he answered without glancing her way again.

"Oh." She was taken a bit by surprise. "I didn't know we would be flying tonight."

"Of course you didn't. I cannot tell you your final destination, because I do not know myself."

"But you'll be flying with me tonight, right now, I mean?" She half hoped he wouldn't be.

"Yes, and that is all I can tell you at this time. Please allow me to continue my surveillance of the area as we drive."

Kaitlin decided she liked that idea, and didn't speak to him again.

In the wee morning hours, they finally boarded a private jet in Cairo, and from the direction of the waning moon in the sky she could see they were heading north toward the Mediterranean.

She was a little nervous because she hadn't considered the relics might have been taken anywhere other than Cairo. There was a small bar on board and she was more than happy to accept a glass of wine from a casually dressed attendant when they were in the air. She must have fallen asleep during the brief flight, because when she woke, they were beginning to land.

Although it was still dark, dawn was near and the smallest sliver of the horizon began to glow. She was fairly certain they were descending into the city of Alexandria, but didn't question her traveling companion. She didn't think he'd answer her.

The plane landed smoothly and the moment it rolled to a stop, her new friend disappeared. It was well past an hour when he returned for her, and then he didn't bother to address her, just motioned for her to exit the plane.

Another car identical to the one she'd ridden in the evening before waited for her at the bottom of the stairs. The sun glinted brightly off the metal of the plane and she squinted against the force of it. The rear passenger side door stood open and she climbed inside, her eyes adjusting to the comparable gloom inside the blackened interior.

"No going through security or anything like that?" she inquired suspiciously and wondered how many bodies were in the trunk.

"You have been cleared and your luggage searched before you

exited the plane."

Kaitlin panicked for a moment and reached inside her jacket to touch the medallion there. It immediately began to radiate warmth. Panos looked at her with shrewd curiosity and she pretended as if she were adjusting the slender belt around her waist.

"I don't suppose you can tell me where we're going this time?" she asked, partly to distract him from his curiosity and partly because she wanted to know.

"We will arrive at the docks shortly," he answered again in his deadpan tone.

"The docks, this time," she mused out loud.

"I look forward to your departure," he said somewhat curtly and stared ahead once more.

"I'm going to miss you too, buddy," she pursed her lips together.

•

The docks were alive with slender white sails gracefully curving in the wind and whispering their gentle promise of adventure.

Kaitlin was thrilled as they drove through the marina, the morning sun sparkling like diamonds off the tiny cresting waves underneath the spectacular display of watercraft.

The car stopped at a pier and she gazed in wonder at a beautiful triple-tiered yacht that flew brilliantly colored flags from many nations. Her pulse quickened and she felt very important to be taken to such a wondrous boat.

She stepped from the car and removed her jacket, letting the salty wind whip through her glossy hair as it caressed her bare shoulders. She slowly walked up to the ramp and turned around to search for her guide.

He stood a little farther down the pier, holding her luggage and smirking in a disquieting manner. She stepped away from the marvelous yacht and moved to join him. He stood directly in front of a run-down fishing boat, and she wasn't sure if perhaps the phrase *run-down* was being a little kind.

"Are you kidding, Panos?" She made a face as the smell of ancient fish guts drifted in her direction.

"I am afraid not, Miss." He smiled with great pleasure, unceremoniously dropping her things onto the dock. "I assure you, I did not make these arrangements."

She regarded his retreating back with no small amount of relief, but that relief faded as she came to realize she was alone on the dock with no one to guide her next steps.

She knew a part of her could be relieved, *should* be relieved, that she had this opportunity to back away from this whole expedition. Her encounter with Panos left shivers running down her spine and she had a difficult time connecting him with the charming Englishman she had come to feel close to during her short time in Egypt.

Kaitlin reached her hand inside her jacket pocket as discreetly as possible, gently caressing the warm metal of the medallion that had led her this far. If she failed now, she would never learn the ancient mysteries of its past or the deepening secrets of her heart.

With a resolve that lifted her spirits and heightened her desires, she stepped one foot onto the softly rolling deck of the fishing boat.

Chapter Four

Though she'd moved a mere two feet from her previous point, Kaitlin felt as if a world had separated her from the shore, her friends and the safety of the familiar.

As she braced herself for anything to happen, the patter of bare feet slapped against the worn wood of the marina dock directly behind her.

She spun to face her new challenge, fully prepared to be strong and defiant in the face of the next unpleasant person she would be forced to deal with. Instead, she squared off with a bucket of rather fresh and pungent fish.

The man behind the catch was a little thin and wiry, she gathered, at least from her view of arms and legs that protruded from behind the pail. Despite herself, she giggled at the unseemly sight of a walking bucket and quickly covered her mouth with her hands, which helped with the stench as well. She was reluctant to let go as the newcomer struggled to set his prize on the dock and extend his own greeting.

Kaitlin extended one hand.

"Lady, I am Mark`het." He grinned and grasped her hand with his brown leather grip, shaking it vigorously. She couldn't help but feel a liking for him as he radiated welcome and awe of her.

"Oh, Lady!" he exclaimed. "Let me help you with your things."

Kaitlin saw her equipment on the dock where Panos had dropped it next to the new bucket of fish.

"Well," she began as tactfully as possible, "I think I can grab this easily if you can get that bucket on board."

"What would Sol say of such a thing?" He chuckled and didn't notice her grimace at the mention of the name. Mark`het swiftly and capably moved all of her items, as well as the fish, onto the small deck of the vessel.

Once Kaitlin stood inside the humble bridge of the fishing boat, she realized the care that had been taken in oiling the ancient wood, the well-worn path of a captain across the deck and the obvious personal touches one could only find in a family-owned vessel. The nets were old, that was true, but they were lovingly patched by hand with a patience that could only denote dedication.

The humble captain of the fishing boat motioned for Kaitlin to sit as he touched the wheel with a proud feel of ownership. She felt a rush of respect for this poor fisherman, a man who obviously felt all the happiness the world he knew had to offer. In a small way, a way she didn't care to consider, she envied him his simple joy for life.

The sun was high in the sky as they went north on the sea and he whistled a small tune that put her at ease on this dangerous venture.

"Mark`het, might I ask you a question?" she began, somewhat unsure of his position in all this and what he might be able to tell her.

"I suppose you might ask me anything." He grinned broadly, his teeth so white against his skin, and his manner confused but willing to please.

"Why don't you tell me about Sol? You must know why I'm here to see him."

"Oh, he says you are here to take pictures, Lady," Mark`het answered. He was clearly torn between affection for her and his loyalty for Sol. "But he did tell me to bring you here with all haste and as politely as I can, which is very polite! I am glad I can help him after all he has done for my family."

His words immediately piqued her interest and she was compelled to ask, "What has he done for your family?"

It was difficult for Kaitlin to imagine what kindness such a tyrant could offer a humble captain of a worn-down ship, but she was eager to learn.

At her question, Mark`het relaxed and she could see he was completely comfortable for the first time since she came on board.

"My brother came to me one day. He spoke to me of a savior, a man who gave him what he needed to care for his family for months. I didn't believe him at first, and that story is sad, but I will say that I came to eventually meet this man and he truly was everything my brother had expressed. He took them from the streets just a short time ago and brought them to his island as honored and trusted staff."

A brief moment of silent contemplation passed and Mark'het sighed as if he had decided to continue with the entire story.

"My brother always tried to do the right thing but the right things did not always happen to him." He smiled to himself and then continued. "He has a beautiful wife and a fine son, but he constantly struggled to give them the life he felt they deserved. So often he became involved in the plots and schemes of ruthless treasure hunters and came close to losing his life, as well as any profit, on most ventures."

He turned to face Kaitlin as he realized she was fully listening to the story. "It was on just such a journey that he met Sol, and though I do not know all the details, he helped him and perhaps even saved his life. I'm sure that he will be happy to tell you the story himself once you reach your destination, but I can say I gladly assist him with the tasks he needs, and I trust him fully."

Kaitlin was speechless, barely daring to hope that her upcoming time with the mysterious Sol could be a time of learning and answers. So little was known of her benefactor, the solitary soul that he was, engaged in the capture of long-lost treasure. Only gossip and hearsay.

Flying along the waves of the Mediterranean, she felt the breeze of survival and her heart lifted as the strength she always drew from her quest for knowledge and adventure flowed through her veins once more.

She began to feel something like her old self again: beautiful, strong and fearless in the face of a newfound discovery. She smiled to herself and thought perhaps her publisher was right and this trip was really what she needed to find her center once more.

The harbor she spied in the distance was a small one, and Kaitlin couldn't discern which port they'd set upon. Mark'het showed concern for her safety as they came near the docks and looked around for a somewhat secluded landing.

"You must stay with my ship, Lady," he instructed her almost apologetically as they drew near to the dock. "This is not the safest of ports, but it is a supply station that is not regulated by any authority and Sol insists everything we do leave no trail. I promise it will not take long to restock this supply list."

Kaitlin was familiar with the temporary ports used by the fine, upstanding associates in the import/export business, and Alexandria in particular was infamous due to its convenient location along the Sea.

She realized the strategic implications of nesting in this area for anonymity and convenience, and at the very least respected Sol for his choice of secret lair locations.

Her skin tingled with excitement at the thought of unmarked treasure, a gathering that must be truly magnificent to warrant such secrecy and care.

The harbor itself was open and safe in the bright sunlight as they came to dock at a vacant space near the end of one floating pier.

People hurried all over the place and Kaitlin hardly imagined anyone took notice of them but realized instantly she was wrong as two burly figures approached the newly arrived vessel. Her heart beat faster in anticipation of anything other than a heartfelt welcome, and indeed though they were granted access, the folded paper money Mark'het slipped into the palm of the lead collector did afford them a small smile at least.

The smaller of the two, though they were both dark-skinned giants to her, looked in her direction with curiosity and sported a different kind of smile. Mark'het grunted gruffly and stepped between his line of sight and Kaitlin, blocking him from her view. A few extra dollars elicited a conciliatory nod and they both walked away.

"Do you see what I mean, Lady?" Markhet asked in genuine concern.

"I know how to be careful." She smiled in return but at the distressed look on his face, spoke again to reassure him. "I will not leave this ship, I promise."

He breathed a sigh of relief and stepped onto the sun-bleached wood of the dock. As he strolled nearly out of her sight, he stopped one last time and turned to see she was well put.

Kaitlin afforded him a small wave and ducked back into the tiny room that served as a bridge. Normally, exploring a shanty town of illegal docks and traders of questionable wares would appeal to her quite a lot, but her mind was focused on the task at hand—and thoughts of Sol and his secrets.

She took a moment to consider the things she'd learned about Sol in contrast to Nigel. Though she felt she knew Nigel well, she also knew he could operate on the shady side of business and up until this point, had no personal experience with Sol.

"Maybe I'll give him a chance to win me over."

She grinned to herself mischievously. It had been so long since Kaitlin felt her own worth, the power of her beauty and character, and the hint of her emotions left her intoxicated and glowing.

"Or perhaps I'll win this mystery man over myself. Why wait, after all?"

She smiled in the solitude of the cabin and reached into her purse to retrieve that long-awaited romance. She realized the absolute attraction passion can hold as she ran her fingers over the cover of the paperback novel—how desire can override all the senses, cause the rise and fall of nations, produce the greatest works of art, even give life or take it away. Such ultimate power it was, the alchemy of love.

As she read the enticing words, she began to lose herself in the story, to believe in fate and destiny. Her bag rested gently on her lap, supporting her book as she flipped through the pages. After a short time, an uncomfortable warmth began to spread to the top of her thighs. The medallion must have been red hot to emanate so much heat through the layers of leather in which it was hidden.

Carefully, she opened her purse and reached inside. Her hand encountered a small, sticky tube and she pulled out a lipstick case covered in thick, creamy paste.

"I should have known this was going to happen," she mumbled.

She fumbling hastily for the actual medallion before it could melt any other necessities. She felt the metal outline of the disc immediately and grabbed it before she realized it wasn't wrapped in the usual layer of soft fabric.

As she frantically pulled it from the bag, the glowing hot metal of the edge she grasped failed to register in her brain immediately, and she completely freed it and swung it out into the open before the searing pain struck.

Her fingers reflexively loosened their grip on the artifact and the momentum of the swing carried it across the room where it smacked against a stained window in the cabin and fell immediately between the wall and the small freezer the captain kept for the more exotic of his catches.

Kaitlin put her fingers in her mouth and nursed her wounds, grumbling under her breath. She was so focused on the pain that she didn't take a moment to retrieve the medallion from its hiding place.

She became aware of a commotion directly outside the boat on the dock. She peeked her head out the door to discern the cause. The two dock workers from the Welcome Wagon stood arguing with their backs to her, right at the edge of the starboard side of the boat.

While their bickering unnerved her slightly, the sight of more money exchanging hands made her much more uneasy. She briefly looked around for a hiding place but there was nothing much bigger than a bread box on board and the fish freezer was right out of the question.

Kaitlin considered quietly slipping over the other side and into the brown, littered water that clung to the harbor, but before she could reach that unpleasant resolution, the two collectors abruptly parted, allowing her a clear view of three clean-cut, tanned gentleman, one of whom was a slender fellow sporting some type of communications handset. The other two were obviously built for harder labor with barrel-sized arms crossed over their massive chests.

She stood and backed into the far corner of the bridge, and that was where they found her as they stepped on deck.

"Doesn't anyone ask for permission to come on board anymore?" she said out loud as the three intruders crowded the small space inside.

"We are going to ask you one time to come with us quietly," the smaller, handsome, olive-skinned spokesman stated flatly.

Kaitlin held no doubt at all that he meant it implicitly, but somewhere her spirit rebelled and in the face of danger she decided to test his resolve.

"My horoscope said I wasn't supposed to take any chances with strangers today," she replied almost casually and was rewarded with a brief look of surprise on the leader's face.

She noticed with some disappointment, his look was replaced with an almost insane glee, a sparkle in his eye that was surely a precursor for insanity or desperation. With an almost imperceptible motion, he gestured to his cohorts who immediately had her pinned helplessly against the wall of the cabin.

He approached her slowly, his handsome face coming just a few short inches from hers. His dark eyes gleamed with a different kind of passion, the kind inspired by madness and this knowledge caused her to shiver involuntarily.

"There is a fine line between chance and fate, my brave girl," he whispered ominously. She felt the cold prick of sharpened steel against her neck just beneath her left ear. "If you are not careful, I will teach you this lesson, though the cost for you will be great indeed."

She cried out sharply as he made his point and warm liquid trickled down her pale, exposed neck. Kaitlin didn't struggle, knowing any resistance would cause the knife to wound her more deeply.

"Shall we walk now?" her captor inquired in an almost conversational manner.

With no choice, she merely nodded with the smallest inclination possible and allowed him to escort her off the boat and onto the forbidden dock. Kaitlin only hoped that Mark'het wouldn't return in time to rush to her defense and foolishly get himself hurt. The thought that the sooner she left the area, the sooner he'd be safe kept her feet moving one in front of the other at a steady pace.

She imagined the silk shirts and tailored clothes of her new friends would arouse a little interest from the locals, but they wisely looked the other way when the entourage passed and Kaitlin realized where she actually was.

She was nowhere—no place anyone would ever look for her.

One sidelong glance to one of her muscle-bound escorts let her know they carried her bag and light jacket, and that led her to believe they were looking for something she had. It stood to reason that something was the medallion and she laughed in spite of her situation as she recalled the freezer on the bridge. Perhaps Fate had called her to school early this day.

•

The shanty town on the small island shone in a kind of squalid splendor that let everyone know an eccentric and eclectic culture of geniuses and thieves populated the area.

It took all kinds to make up the business ventures that displayed "export" in their titles and encompassed everyone from the desperate, honest archaeologist who needed to study that one inaccessible find, to the lowly grave robbers who hung about like vultures waiting for the sale of a lifetime.

Morals and values fell into very different and personal categories when history and treasure were concerned. So Kaitlin found herself escorted through an illegal city built by lust, greed and passion of all sorts—and somewhere amidst the chaos and fear she knew she was closer to the answers she sought and accepted her fate readily.

The needle didn't really bother her. For some reason needles never made her squeamish, but the liquid inside the vial burned as it entered her veins, leaving her with a nauseated feeling in the pit of her stomach.

"I prefer it this way, you know," the handsome stranger whispered as he faced her inside the small, dark room she'd been taken to. "Your face is far too lovely to mar," he added almost wistfully and sat back in the chair opposite her. "You will tell me what you know, of course, and everything will be fine."

His voice came at her from a distance, almost soothing, and she felt herself relax. A small sound escaped her lips and caused her captor to lean forward and curiously regard her. The motion of his movement flowed over her in hot waves and her perception was distorted to the point she didn't bother to try to make out any of the details. She saw him stand abruptly and snap his fingers at the burly attendants.

"You gave her too much." His soft tone drifted out accusingly, and the accomplices stepped back in a blur of panic.

Kaitlin couldn't restrain the peal of delighted laughter that escaped her lips and had no reflex reaction at all as his hand shot forward to silence her. She fully expected a sharp slap across mouth but was surprised as his fingertips rested gently against her full lips.

"Such extraordinary beauty, really." He breathed in the type of reverence reserved only for the truly, passionately mad. His voice dropped lower, became more intimate as he spoke directly to her. "When I photographed you in Cairo, I thought you stunning. Yet the presence of your spirit casts you in a far greater light and I find that fascinating."

"Lucien, now is not the time for your distractions," a new voice stated sternly from the shadows, shadows that had grown considerably since her arrival. The edges of her vision were blurred, darkened past the normal absence of light that filled the corners of the confining shack.

The distant sound of water lapped gently in waves beneath her and she knew she was not far from the boat. She tried to orient herself with the ambient sounds around her. The drug was powerful and her vision grew weaker as it flowed more freely through her veins.

"She is useless to us now," the intoxicating, smooth voice of her interrogator cut through the murky depths of her awareness. "If she is damaged in any way I will not be pleased."

"The item is not with her things." The newcomer cut in again, asserting his authority over the situation. "I am certain she was in possession of it earlier."

He seemed hauntingly familiar to Kaitlin, but she couldn't

place him without a look at his face, and that opportunity was unlikely after the newcomer's next gruff order.

"If it is not with her or on her, then we have lost it. I do not appreciate this type of error in judgment from my partners. Have it in hand before I return."

It may have been her imagination, but the room grew slightly less overwhelming and the air was easier to breathe after the newcomer left.

"You seem to have lost something recently, Dove," Lucien began in that soothing yet dangerous tone as he softly stroked the silky skin of her flushed cheek. "Perhaps you can tell me what it is, so we can get this unpleasant business over with. Everything will be better, after you tell me."

His voice reassured, but she was unsteady and confused, losing touch with the reality of what was happening to her now. It was true that she had no control over her emotions at the moment, no control over the things she said and his urging words did guide her.

"It'll be better?" she asked in a hopeful voice, her blue eyes staring directly into his.

"Oh," he said softly, gazing deeply at her, "when I am finished, I will move the earth and the stars to make the world a better place for you."

There was something in his voice, a tremor, a moment of intense honesty that Kaitlin believed in her soul. She no longer remembered where she was, no longer held any thoughts of her present situation. Only the past prevailed at the forefront of her mind and heart.

A deep tear, flowing from her soul, spilled from her eye and in those few moments she couldn't breathe. Her captor leaned dangerously close, his breath on her skin like a foreign breeze against the contours of her face.

"Share with me your secrets," he whispered as he seemingly drew out her emotions, her very essence.

"I lost Alex." Her tears came freely. "I had him with me and I kept care of his heart and I let him go. I lost Alex."

"Incredible," he breathed out the word as he regarded her devastated face. "Her greatest secret, her most valuable treasure is not gold, not gems. It is a broken heart."

"She is crying," one of the brawny men stated uncomfortably. "What does that mean?"

"It means she is a far better person than you, my thick friend."

"We are all here for the same thing," the accomplice angrily replied, disliking this turn of events.

"We may be here for the same thing," Lucien assented soothingly to calm the ruffled man's offended ego. "But we are not here for the same reason. You are along for the explicit promise of wealth, maybe even fame. I could never presume to instruct you as to my purpose."

The larger man took a moment to let the words sink in and eventually decided they were probably not an insult. "What do we do with the girl, then?"

"I will take care of you, Dove," Lucien answered to Kaitlin instead, almost tenderly as he turned his full attention back to her. She was barely lucid, lost in a sea of her own memories.

"Why do you call her Dove?" The big man spat out in frustration, probably rethinking his role in the entire event.

"Look at her, Sir," he answered with a gesture. "She shines like the midnight sun. She will be my guiding light on this journey we undertake. There are many forms of treasure, gentlemen. You should learn the value of things such as her. Now, we go to the dock and search the boat."

His companions lingered at the small wooden door as if unsure of his orders.

"What are we going to do with her while we do that?" The smaller of the two nodded in her direction, finally mustering enough nervous courage to question his motives.

Lucien sighed and said carefully, "When I say 'we,' gentlemen, I mean to illustrate to you our next move as an organization. The two of you will search the craft while I monitor the woman. As you were so kind to point out to me earlier, we have a common goal and we are working together toward it in earnest cooperation."

They both shuffled their feet a bit uncomfortably and waited for him to continue.

"You do recall, of course, reminding me of the reason we are here, do you not?" His voice took on a darkened tone and his accent became thicker.

Kaitlin thought his accent might be of a Middle Eastern nature, though it was so filled with venom it was difficult to discover anything other than his ire at the moment. She had difficulty holding her head up on her own and her hands were tied behind the chair.

Yet even as her captors discussed the present situation, her head became clearer and she was able to understand the more subtle things happening around her. She dipped her head lower and watched through a veil of hair, determined to be strong and discover whatever she could.

She smiled behind her shield, privately regarding the irony of her situation. She had finally spoken her greatest secret out loud and the desperately sad images that haunted her for so long were replaced by memories she was resolved to treasure of her time with Alex.

She was lost in thought so deeply that she didn't notice she was alone in the room with her interrogator. He regarded her with a look of almost wonder on his face, and a deep curiosity one might reserve for a rare exhibit unveiled for the first time to an adoring audience.

"Tell me, Dove—" His words were so tender and soft, and enough of the drug was in her system at just the right time that she felt unable to resist his forthcoming question. She attempted to steel her will against his and set her jaw as he came closer.

" —tell me why you smile in such a way."

Kaitlin was momentarily stunned by his inquiry, but in her confused state she meant to answer him honestly, as if he were her closest friend and confidant in the world.

"Our lives are not made up of the things we possess," she began, raising her head fully and looking into his deep dark eyes, seeing emptiness there, a longing for something he'd never fulfilled. "We must always take the experiences we have, that mean the most to us, and turn them into something beautiful to hang in the gallery of our soul. Not everything that happens to us in life is fair and sometimes it's very painful. We can either choose the beauty or horror."

"And what do you choose?" he asked, as if he expected her to have all the answers.

"I choose to take my experiences and make them into something I can love and keep close to my heart. I choose to be inspired so that I may inspire others."

He hovered close to her face as she answered, his warm breath glossing over her skin. For a moment she felt pressure on her lips and thought he might have even kissed her.

"You will, of course, teach me to feel this way." He pulled back as if recovering his senses and began to pace around the shack. The boards protested in a near symphony of creaks and groans as he walked a path around her chair, deep in thought.

"Not everything can be taught by one person," she reminded him, a hint of pain in her tone as she attempted to flex her bound hands.

He was instantly aware of the tremor in her voice and stepped behind the chair. Kaitlin was uncomfortable with him out of her line of sight and braced herself for the cold touch of steel against her skin that would surely be a sign of his displeasure at her comment.

In one breathless moment, he released her from her bonds, though she could not discern if it was freedom by the knife, or a simple locking mechanism.

She rubbed her tender wrists in an effort to revive the circulation to her hands and made as if to stretch her neck as she captured a few furtive glances of the area in which she was ensconced.

Night was obviously upon them because the sunlight no longer filtered through the cracks of the poorly constructed shanty. The waves that gently lapped beneath her earlier sounded much more aggressive and her guardian grew agitated. He spun about abruptly as the door crashed open and his two accomplices entered breathlessly.

"It's gone," the unfortunate spokesman panted. He took two steps backward at the look Lucien afforded him.

"What is gone?" he asked with visible restraint.

Both men backed through the small doorway and onto the actual dock before they answered.

"The boat that brought her here?" The larger one answered in the form of a question, as if it were possibly something he could guess right.

Kaitlin's heart beat faster and she was relieved at the thought her friend Mark'het had gotten away to safety.

Lucien afforded no such generous allowances as he spoke his next words. "There are two docking lines to search?" He raised an eyebrow.

"Yes, two," the tall partner answered instantly. "Though we have already searched part of the eastern landing."

"How many do we number in our party?" he again calmly inquired.

"Three, of course," the giant of a man said then took a moment to consider his answer.

He looked up in surprise, his mouth forming a wide "O" when Kaitlin's newfound confidant attacked. One small, quick movement lodged his knife deeply into the offending henchman's jugular vein. He immediately fell inside the wooden shack, halfway through the door.

"That's lucky," her once compassionate captor commented to the remaining thug. "All you have to do now is drag him the rest of the way through."

It didn't take long before the surviving member of the party got the body through the door and into the corner.

Tears streamed down Kaitlin's face. She'd seen enough death to last her a lifetime.

"Surely you do not weep for one who would have treated you so callously," her kidnapper said gently.

"I weep for all lost life," she spat out bitterly in his direction as a look of surprise passed his face.

"Such spirit you have," he said with a look of twisted admiration. He added as an afterthought, "This too, you will teach me. I never thought to meet one such as you in our profession. I assume you will search the remainder of the eastern dock?" he inquired of the man still standing over the slouched figure of his former partner in the corner.

He shrugged in assent and in a gesture that surprised Kaitlin, reached down and closed the eyes of his fallen comrade. It reminded her that everyone lives in a separate and unique universe. To that man, a man she might even compare to Mark'het's brother, his world and the importance of it existed solely for him and his family and the people in his sphere of reality.

Kaitlin's hands and ankles were bound again.

"You will wait here for me, yes?" Lucien spoke over his shoulder as he exited the room, not waiting for any reply.

She considered that he didn't gag her. He wouldn't be very far from their location. Even if she chose to cry out, it was doubtful anyone other than him would come.

The waves crashed strongly against the supporting piers of wood beneath, which protested quite loudly. She nearly cried out as a portion of the wood flooring gave way just below her feet, but managed to hold her tongue.

In no time at all, a manhole-sized opening appeared and Mark'het pulled himself up into the room.

"No, you have to go back and save yourself," she cautioned with a whisper.

He only grinned and released her from her bonds in a few short seconds. "I know how to rescue fair damsels in distress," he assured her as he dropped back into the hole almost as abruptly as he appeared.

Kaitlin stood a little numbly, regarding the means of his exit when a brown hand, followed by an arm, shot swiftly through.

"Come on," his friendly voice urged.

With no other thought she jumped directly into the opening. Fortunately, she landed inside a small rowboat. Mark'het gave her a brief hug and motioned for his cohorts to row. With absolutely no sound, they skimmed the water underneath the makeshift marina and breached the dock completely.

Kaitlin expected to see the boat docked on the nearby pier, but it was a few leagues out, anchored she would guess, against the mounting waves.

"A storm is coming, Lady," Mark'het cautioned her as an enthusiastic spray washed over everyone on board.

"I've seen it," she answered cryptically. She gratefully wrapped a woolen blanket around herself.

When they boarded his ship, she still couldn't shake the chill of her captor's touch or the intent of his words. It was only from exhaustion that she allowed herself to sleep once on board the familiar fishing vessel.

•

The sun shone through her eyelids, coating her dreams in a bright red she didn't care to regard that early in the morning. She was immediately greeted by a relieved looking captain.

"Good morning, my friend. As you can see, we have nearly arrived. Once you are safely on the island, my brother will see to all your needs."

Kaitlin followed his look to regard her final destination. There were probably many crumbling yet formidable, fortresses on deserted islands in the Mediterranean, but she couldn't have guessed which one she was approaching.

She gathered from the position of the sun in the sky they'd traveled just a short amount of time before they saw the structure in the distance. The stone walls were grey and crumbling, and gave her a chill to see from even a far-off vantage.

The base of the garrison was surrounded by huge a outcropping of rocks, making it look fairly difficult to get near. But the boat glided quietly into an almost-hidden cove and through a narrow waterway that actually led underneath the keep.

As they tied to a small platform that allowed the landing of only one craft, she noticed in the cold and clammy underbelly of the fortress that the only way up was through a solid iron gate with a huge lock.

Mark'het held a modern, electric lantern aloft as they ascended the complicated and winding stone stairwell into the keep itself. Though the fixtures on the walls hinted at the fact the place was wired with electricity, she was intrigued by the original iron sconces that still marked the way along the corridors. Their rust color tears ran down the stone and wept for her the stories of ages past and battles that may never be told.

Still groggy from her dock-side experience, she was glad to lean on the fishing captain's arm as her bags were carried behind by people that she could only describe as relatives of her new friend, they so resembled one another.

As she progressed farther from the boat, a moment of panic crossed her face and she remembered what occurred the previous day.

"Mark'het, may I have a moment alone on your ship? I'm in

a new place and suddenly overwhelmed. I may feel at my most comfortable in familiar surroundings."

He immediately regarded her with concern, but motioned for their entourage to move forward without them.

"I will give you whatever you need, Lady. I am sorry for the things you have been through and I will do whatever I can to make you happy."

Kaitlin smiled as he led her back through the twisted corridors and onto the small boat, which tossed in the waves.

"Could you give me a moment?"

"I shall go on ahead and await your arrival at the top of the landing." He beamed in his solution. "Should you need anything at all please call out to me."

Kaitlin nodded her gratitude and went inside the bridge. She still held the lantern, and smiled at the gallant way Mark'het held aloft his Zippo lighter as he progressed up the stone stairwell.

It was no time at all before she found the medallion wedged behind the freezer. It offered no resistance as she pulled it free and tucked it inside her pocket. It wasn't as if she didn't trust her new friend. However, she now knew the danger of their situation and was unwilling to cause any unnecessary harm to anyone by burdening them with knowledge that could be used against them.

"That's right, isn't it?" she asked of the relic in an offhanded way, and set course after Mark'het who was quite relieved to see her when she breached the top of the stairs.

She was pleasantly surprised to discover her room was comfortable and accommodating after her short-lived escort through the passages of the archaic stone edifice.

It seemed no time at all before Mark'het reappeared, rapping lightly at her door.

"The master of the house requests your presence for dinner this evening, if you are feeling well," he said.

She smiled in response, as much not to offend him as to accept this loathsome dinner invitation.

Unhappy with spending that much of an evening with a man she was inclined to despise, she dressed rather plainly for the event. When Mark'het returned to escort her, she was glad for his company but slowed her pace as he informed her they approached the dining hall.

The heavy, polished doors stood open and glistened as the firelight sparkled off their ancient surface. Her friend took his leave with a slight bow and a smile, and was gone in absolute silence down the stone corridor.

Kaitlin was suddenly fearful of meeting this stranger, this man of whom she'd heard so many stories, so she remained just outside the warmth of the dining room in the cold, unforgiving stone corridor. A cool sea breeze drifted down the passage and she shivered, forcing her to take a step inside.

She could see the tall figure of a dark-haired man standing with his back to her in front of the warm fireplace. She felt a rush of nervous fluttering deep in her stomach as he turned to face her, and she was stunned to see the person standing before her.

"Greetings, M'Lady," Solaus said in a warm, exotic voice.

He took two steps toward her, the stranger from the airport—the man of her dreams.

At first she couldn't breathe and wanted to reach out to him, but then she remembered the things Nigel said and lowered her head. As a result, she didn't see the almost anguished and tormented passion in his eyes as he first regarded her.

Chapter Five

Kaitlin desperately attempted to regain control of her breathing, to assert some semblance of calm into her demeanor. But her stomach felt as if a thousand butterflies had taken flight inside and drained the very essence from her being.

Solaus appeared to brace himself against the light of the fire, but his deep blue eyes blazed with longing. Moments passed, though Kaitlin had no gauge to measure how many, when her mysterious stranger crossed the room to stand before her.

"Thank you for allowing me to come tonight." She grasped for any words she could find as she quickly lifted her face to regard him fully. Her cheeks were flushed and hot, her lips slightly parted from labored breathing. He seemed stunned, unable to look away from her rapt expression.

"I knew you were coming," he stated in a barely audible whisper, "yet I had no idea how much I needed you until now."

The grey, woolen shawl Kaitlin had wrapped around herself to ward away the chill of the seaside halls slipped from her shaky grasp and she was unable to catch it as it fell to the cold floor. Though she had only donned a simple, well-worn tank top and jeans before the meeting, her skin burned with an inner fire that could feel nothing of the breeze.

"Allow me, Kaitlin." He reached with ease to capture the wayward wrap. Hearing her name spoken by him in those lush, passionate tones, sent a deep shiver up her spine.

He immediately mistook her uncontrolled response as a sign of discomfort and lifted the cloak over her head, allowing it to drape across her shoulders. The cool, white silk of his sleeve brushed against her bare skin for just a moment and she leaned against his arm, unable to bear parting with his touch.

Solaus sighed as if any remnant of self-control he might have possessed was forever lost. His free arm encircled her delicate waist and he pulled her to him roughly, desire surpassing any caution he may have tried to keep in place.

Kaitlin gasped as her body was crushed against his lean, hard frame. She breathed in his scent—the rich, heady oils of the orient as she flung her wrap to the floor once again.

His strong, urging hands slowly moved up the small of her back and she clung to him with a need more powerful than any she had ever known. His fingers fanned out across the back of her neck and entwined in her hair as he gently but firmly used the leverage to pull her head back and gaze into her eyes. She hungered for the taste of his lips as they hovered close.

"I need to be here with you, too," she responded to his earlier statement, her voice glossy and heavy with lust.

"Yes." He smiled slightly as his mouth grew near. "But you come highly recommended. Who might tell you about me?"

Instantly it seemed as if those words cooled his passion, for as soon as he spoke them, his eyes grew clearer and he released his grasp of her.

"I nearly forgot." He stepped back slowly and his tone grew distant. "You come highly recommended."

"I don't understand." Kaitlin nearly stumbled at his withdrawal, her body still screaming for his touch while her mind backpedaled in confusion.

"I doubt that," he replied stonily, returning to his original position in front of the large fire.

Her confusion and grief at his harsh accusation must have

shone clearly on her face, and the hot tears of utter rejection ran down her now frosty cheeks.

She felt as if every molecule of warmth had been drained from her body as her eyes were inexorably drawn to the dashing figure of the man who seemed to possess her very soul. Though the fire cast him in shadow, his defiant thoughts were vibrantly written across his ruggedly attractive face.

His swollen lips, so close to hers just moments before, were pressed together in a hard resolve, like his strong jaw. His arms were crossed over his chest, the white silk straining against the firm definition of his biceps. His tight black slacks fit him like a glove and he stood with his legs spread slightly apart, feet planted firmly on the stone. It seemed he was prepared to withstand the greatest of tempests that might dare attempt to sway his position.

Kaitlin's mind raced for a reason that his treatment should be so callous, but in her state there was nothing she could see. There were few words to describe the way she felt at his touch and the agony of his withdrawal, only that perhaps her heart was alight with a thousand candles for the first time in her life and she could see the true, beautiful image of her being reflected in his eyes. And then Fate chose to blow out the candles, leaving her in a darkness more profound than any she would have known if she had not just experienced such illumination.

The tears fell freely from her eyes then, a mixture of emotions that owed their allegiance to her ordeal on the dock, her acceptance of the loss of Alex, and this newfound passion that felt as if it had been present since the beginning of time.

She buried her face deeply in the shawl, pressing it tightly against her mouth in an attempt to cover any distressing sounds. A random sob broke free from her defense and Solaus dropped his hands to his side as his armor broke even its most determined hold.

She didn't see him step softly forward, his right arm extended tentatively with fingers reaching to comfort her against his better judgment.

The flame crackled in the grate of the huge stone fireplace and Kaitlin swayed slightly with the same displaced feeling she'd experienced on the airplane. She gently rubbed her eyelids with her fingertips and was surprised to feel silky smooth cloth instead of wool pressed against her delicate skin.

"Come forward." She heard a commanding voice from the great distance, farther than the length of the dining hall they were in.

Slowly she dropped her hands from her face to regard the pale white fingers that grasped a hand-blown vial. Very carefully, she glanced down the length of her body, all of it covered in a luxurious drape of satin and silk, and knew instinctively that her hair and face were also covered in a like fashion. Only her eyes would be visible.

The room extended to what must probably have been the length of the keep itself. On each side, a row of massive stone columns lined the obvious procession way to the end of the hall. She was surprised to find that none of this was shocking to her; it felt like a dream she'd had many times.

It didn't take long for her to realize she was counting her steps, pacing her forward glide in a seamless flow of movement. Just as she knew the pace forward, she was aware of five other girls behind her, all under the same training, all wearing the required costume for this important moment.

At the very edge of her hearing, the whispers of the Matron Mothers followed them down the path as they stood anxiously wringing their hands and watching just out of sight. Kaitlin knew only the most beautiful vessels were chosen to serve the acolytes in the great Temple of Atar, just as she knew the politics that went hand-in-hand with the ceremony of choosing she now participated in. After all, she'd spent her entire young life preparing for this very moment.

Many young men from noble houses were sent to serve at the temple; it was quite fashionable for them to speak of the accomplishments of their education and training in the faith. Though it was never a spoken philosophy, it often occurred that upon fulfilling their duty to society, these young men retained the services of their temple companions as concubines. No union past that could ever be expected by those with the divine responsibilities of royalty, but the girls were always very grateful to achieve that station alone. Many of the hopeful serving maidens were orphans or very low-class citizens who might never aspire to such a match.

It felt to Kaitlin like she had rehearsed this a thousand times, that she knew every step, yet her apprehension and excitement for the moment were overwhelming and nothing outside this dream existed.

She knew she was strikingly beautiful, yet her hands tensed against the delicate glass of her offering to the acolytes, for though she was lovely beyond measure, she saw her world through the deepest of blue eyes, an unusual quality that her people either prized or disdained. And at this moment of choosing, she feared greatly because the whole of her worth would be presented through her eyes.

Indeed, her Matron Mother had taken a great chance in selecting her as her charge, for her very own future depended on Kaitlin—wherever her young student lived out her life would be the fate of her mentor as well.

Though a thousand steps or more passed beneath her delicate feet, she instinctively knew she'd reached the edge of the altar platform itself, and took her appointed position at the far left end with her head lowered as each forthcoming girl fanned out along the circular dais.

Impressive fires burned in huge braziers along the back of the marble platform and Kaitlin kept her eyes properly cast downward as she regarded the stone carvings along the edge. A masterful artisan sculptor must have worked day and night to create the magnificent bronze and silver panels embedded along the stonework that depicted the worshipers bestowing divine gifts upon the fire god himself.

A sharp snap instantly brought her out of her reverie and she knew the time was at hand. Each hopeful candidate gazed upward on command as the first acolyte stepped onto the dais. He carefully regarded each woman before moving along the line, pausing a moment before each contender, then nodding his respect before moving on.

He came to Kaitlin at the end and she was unable to restrain the slightest tremble as he regarded her veiled face. She waited for the look of surprise that would surely cross his young features, but instead he seemed almost quizzical and moved back to the first candidate at the opposite end.

In a moment of obvious respect and awe for the girl he had chosen, he stepped lightly off the platform and bowed low before her, cupping both his hands together, palms up, to accept her sacred essence. Her eyes were wide and full of joy at being chosen first and she softly set the unique bottle designed solely for her, filled with Myrrh, into his grasp.

The squeal of delight from the far end of the chamber was difficult to ignore, and the first girl smiled beneath her veil, turning back the way she'd come. She was free to move about the temple then, as her new station allowed her the license to conduct business without question for her new master.

As each acolyte came among them and made his choice, their ranks grew thinner and Kaitlin was left with her closest comrade; a quiet girl of dark and frail beauty.

"Anaya," Kaitlin whispered as forthrightly as she dared in their situation, hoping to lend her friend strength and perhaps comfort herself a small amount as well.

She glanced over to see the delicate, porcelain hands of the girl gripping her own decanter in anguish. She could nearly smell the cinnamon essence inside.

Anaya was chosen because her skin shone like the light of the moon in all its bright and pale perfection. She was the kindest of people Kaitlin had ever known and deep inside her heart she wished for her friend to be chosen because she feared for her delicate constitution and shy, fragile disposition.

Again came the attentive snap and they both looked with hope and wonder on the newcomer. He was taller than the rest, graceful and agile in his movements, and there was a dark beauty to his features that caused both girls to count their wishes.

With no regard to decorum, he lightly jumped off the platform to stand boldly in front of the remaining women. He looked immediately to Kaitlin, the taller of the two, but she saw in his eyes what she had so often seen in others—he immediately discounted her as flawed and turned to Anaya.

With an almost mocking shrug, he held out his hands and waited with barely restrained patience for her to deposit the symbol of her essence. When she did so, he grabbed it up immediately and tossed it into the air twice, causing both women to flinch. Without so much as a backward look, he caught it and turned on his heel, leaving the audience chamber.

Anaya raised her eyes to Kaitlin's in a fleeting moment of panic, but her friend reassured her as best she could without words, urging her forward with the most subtle inclination of her head. It was as much as she dared to do, as she resumed her solitary position in front of the temple master.

She didn't need to see the pitying look on his face as he glanced her way. It was well known among the girls that should the last hopeful remain unchosen, she could very well end up on the streets with no master or protection.

Though she was forced by role to keep her eyes lowered, she squared off her shoulders and held her strength deep inside, felt nothing of the despair she should have been drowning in. It was far better she be left behind than her fragile friend, and she was more than willing to accept her fate.

A last step fell directly before her and she stoically awaited the order to remove herself from the hall.

"This is highly unheard of," the unmistakable temple master's voice dripped with disapproval above her head, and she tended to agree.

"I mean to do this." A deep, exotic voice answered him and there was no mistaking the resolve behind his tones. "Unless you wish to take this up with my father, of course?"

The resounding gasp from the alcove filled with curious Matrons sent a chill through her veins. She was deeply, profoundly shaken but could feel no reason that anything other than relief would occupy her. Surely, any match was better than none for her chaperone and poor family.

"It is the Prince." A muffled cry came from the back hall, as someone obviously attempted to restrain her outburst.

Before Kaitlin could process the highly volatile words, the snap came once more. Nervous this time, she looked up from pure reflex.

Solaus stood before her, the fires of Atar blazing behind him. The impact of the realization that he was the prince to the throne of the entire kingdom was lessened only by the gaze of his deep blue eyes into hers.

She instantly felt as if her body had become lighter than air, and her legs disappeared entirely. She was surprised when she sunk to the floor instead of rising to the heavens.

Without a moment of hesitation, Solaus leapt to the floor and by gesture alone asked her permission to touch her and assist her to rise.

The only reply available to her was a wordless nod of assent, which she gave with no thought to her position, or his. He gallantly reached forward and wrapped his strong hands around her tiny wrists, his fingers momentarily resting against her pulse point where he allowed them to linger for a fraction of a second.

Once she was upright and steady on her feet, he smiled in a way that would forever blind her soul to any other intentions, and went down on one knee before her.

A multiple number of thuds were clearly audible from the hidden alcove, but neither of the ardent young people took notice. The Temple Master's hand gripped the stem of a brazier until his knuckles were white, but he uttered no words of dissent.

Her royal acolyte held his palms together, tightly closed like a new lotus bloom, and then spread his hands wide before her in the ceremonial gesture.

Kaitlin took her vial of sandalwood oil, the very scent applied to her at birth, and gave it to him, knowing she willingly gave her heart as well. She accepted this as readily as she knew the day would dawn anew the first thing tomorrow.

It was quite a while before she realized the back of her hands remained cradled in his upright palms far longer than propriety would have allowed, and as this registered in her eyes, a deep blush spread across the divine cheeks of the Prince because he knew he'd allowed it.

"Lady?" A hesitant voice reached her ears and she was quite unwilling to let go of the dream, of his hands, as the fire crackled in the distance.

"Please, are you feeling well?" The concerned tone invaded her moment of absolute bliss and she shook her head to ward it off.

The unfortunate shake cleared her mind and she opened her eyes to regard Mark'het standing very near her and Solaus, his face strained in worry.

A brief inspection of the situation released her willing hands from Sol's gentle placement and she could see from one furtive glance into his eyes that he was as swayed as she by the occurrence.

"This cannot be happening," she assured herself under her breath as she began to pace the length of the dining table, much to the concern of Mark'het.

He stepped up to her path and set a calming hand on her arm. She looked up at him, still a little lost in the memory of the vision she had just experienced, but accepted his offer to be seated as he pulled out her chair.

The table was rectangular and not overly long, though it could easily seat twelve people. Mark'het cast an obvious frown in Sol's brooding direction, and he shrugged defensively.

The air was thick with tension as Sol seated himself opposite her. Blue and white lotus blossoms floated in a mismatched array of gold and ceramic bowls all along the settings. The dishes and silverware that adorned the table were magnificent and had a thrown-together look, but Kaitlin regarded them in appreciation and was impressed by their eclectic design.

"My brother, Drosk, tells me Mister Solaus did not approve of the serving ware we use on an everyday basis, and had him search the reserve for finer things you might dine on." Mark'het chuckled a little when Sol gave him an uncomfortable look.

"The treasure room, I mean the reserve, is a mess right now." A hearty voice joined in the conversation as another person entered the dining hall behind her.

When the man came into view, Kaitlin knew he must be Mark'het's brother, for they were very similar in age and manner. He carried a bottle of wine wrapped in a linen towel, and that was something she appreciated more than just about any other gesture at the moment.

"I am Drosk," he offered, lightly pouring a dark, red liquid into her cup. "How do you like your fine glass?" He laughed as she lifted the warm metal to her lips. "This could be the cup of Christ, for all we know, yet you are most welcome to use it!"

"Then I shall live forever," she declared as she took a deep draught and looked into Sol's eyes over the rim of the handcrafted work of art.

She caught him looking back at her intensely, though his gaze shifted the moment she discovered him. The heavy metal of the cup was quite weighty in her grasp and she reluctantly set it and its contents on the table. She smiled inwardly as she noticed most of her silverware matched, though one knife was silver and the fork was embedded with tiny gemstones.

"This setting is a great treasure, indeed," she assured Drosk, who beamed at his accomplishment.

Kaitlin was so very grateful for the presence of Mark'het and his brother, because nothing of what she expected was happening on this assignment. Apparently, she'd only be able to learn about her host through the people close to him. He obviously intended to push her away and though she longed to find the reasons she felt the way she did, she'd be foolish to expose herself to him after he clearly declined her heart.

As lost in thought as she was, she was unable to mistake the sound of excited shuffling in the corridor. It was a small scuff at first, but it grew with frequency as someone carried on their conversation.

"Now?" an impatient inquiry was issued from the outer hallway as Kaitlin turned to try to discover the source of the disembodied voice.

Drosk rolled his eyes dramatically but with a knowing smile, and nodded his head in the direction of the hall.

With a smile that stretched from ear to ear, a child no older than the one she'd encountered at the airport slowly entered the dining room. He held in front of him, as reverently as a child can dream of, a handful of blue lotus blooms, which he set on the left side of her plate.

"May I introduce to you, kind lady," Drosk began with exaggeration, surely what the child wished for, "my son Develin."

Kaitlin was instantly struck by the resemblance between the

child at the airport and the one standing before her, and deeply touched once more by the generosity Solaus had shown that wayward boy she met on her arrival.

And no wonder she couldn't help but think to herself. *Drosk's son is so similar. Sol must be very fond of this child.*

"I apologize for not meeting you when you arrived earlier this morning." Drosk put an arm around his boy as he came to his side. "Develin wished very much to go to the mainland and pick for you these flowers personally."

Develin grinned and looked away from her, but she could see his quick glance toward the lotus filled vessels all along the table and knew the display was his handiwork.

"Come here." She reached out a hand to the boy and he shook his head, blushing furiously. Drosk did his best to hide the laughter in his tone as he addressed her formally.

"My son has been on pins and needles ever since he heard you would be arriving. We do not meet many fine ladies in our line of work and his shy nature was superseded by his excitement."

The small child looked up at his father in earnest. "Except for Mother, of course!"

Drosk looked down at his son with such pride and love that it took Kaitlin's breath away. "Your Mother is an angel from above, and I thank the Host of Heaven for every day she is with us on our journey."

"Tomorrow you will meet her, Lady," Develin assured her, and she was truly honored to look forward to the introduction. "And until we meet again." His small, delicate face took on an almost serious nature and he slowly approached her, gently taking her hand. His young, dark eyes held hers and he raised the back of her fingers to his lips, kissing them in an exaggerated fashion.

Kaitlin was shocked by his behavior and the room filled with the laughter of all the men present.

"They learn so quickly these days," Sol commented affectionately, though Kaitlin believed she heard the slightest tone of envy in his voice. The boy held his composure as long as he could, though his cheeks burned red with sensitivity. It didn't take long before he disappeared from their presence.

"Let us take our leave as well," Mark'het said, though he cast an uncertain look in Sol's general direction.

"I assure you, I can manage the safety and wellbeing of our new guest," Solaus stated dryly, and both brothers hid a grin as they exited the room.

Though Kaitlin would have thought food was the farthest thing from her mind, she realized the smell of flame-broiled chicken and vegetables coming from underneath the slightly tarnished silver platters on the table before her was as intoxicating as the wine.

With a quick glance to make sure Drosk had left the bottle of alcohol, she reached forward to uncover her dinner.

There was a small hen, perhaps a quail on the plate in front of her, and the potatoes and carrots steamed their delicious aroma in tantalizing waves before her nose. Nestled within the vegetables was a small terra-cotta bowl filled with large, fresh cloves of roasted garlic.

Her stomach protested loudly at the delay and she looked around innocently to see if her dinner companion had noticed. He merely leaned with one elbow on the thick oak table, his strong, square chin supported between his thumb and fingers as he regarded her. Subconsciously perhaps, his fingers stroked his lips in contemplation.

Kaitlin was mesmerized by his actions and completely overtaken by the desire to rise from her seat and cross the length of the table, sit upon his lap and leave the devil to care as she covered his sensuous lips with her own. Before she realized the direction of her movements, she had actually stood and walked to the side of the table.

With her blue eyes locked onto his, searching for any sign of emotion, she stretched forth an arm and took hold of the wine bottle.

"Oh, here it is," she whispered softly. "Just what I was looking for."

"Was it?" he inquired in the same quiet tone as she took the wine from the bucket and backed into her chair. She made a good show of pouring quite a large amount into the cup when in fact it was nearly full to begin with.

"I hope this vintage is to your liking. I had it brought in specifically for you." His words alone were seductive and inviting.

She lifted the heavy goblet and allowed a small amount to glide through her lips and onto her tongue. She had a habit of savoring the taste as long as possible before allowing it to continue on its way.

"I see you are a connoisseur." He smiled approvingly. "Keep it in your mouth for as long as you desire. Develop the taste completely before swallowing it entirely."

Kaitlin was hardly sure she could breathe let alone swallow, but her empty stomach demanded she proceed.

"I am certain you must be famished. Please do not do Drosk the disservice of declining his lovingly prepared meal."

"Pop Tarts," she exclaimed, suddenly realizing when she had eaten last and greatly lightening the mood as a result.

Solaus laughed out loud at her outburst. "Surely Mark'het did not part with his prized breakfast delicacy for even such a worthy recipient of yourself?"

"He tells me he gets a great deal on American Pop Tarts from eBay," Kaitlin assured him a little defensively.

"Perhaps he did afford you one such delicate pastry, but I know he could never have parted with his Apple Cinnamon for anyone," he joked, clearly urging her on, but curious nonetheless at the length his comrade would go to for this woman.

"I don't suppose you'll ever know," she answered smugly and allowed the glow of one small victory to wash over her that evening.

He crossed his silken clad arms across his chest once again, not even making the pretense of glancing at his food anymore as he stared directly at her.

"It certainly was a good Pop Tart," she commented as she cut into her bird, pulling part of the breast away and slipping the hot, juicy meat into her mouth.

Her host stood abruptly and approached her with an easy stride, his muscular legs flexing with each step. Kaitlin froze with her latest bite in her mouth as he came quite near.

"You will beg my pardon, of course," he said with great propriety.

With one strong hand, he reached underneath the great wooden table. Neither drew breath or made a sound as he hovered there looking directly into her eyes. With one fluid motion, he took hold of the linen napkin on her lap and brought it forth.

No words were spoken as he took the fine fabric and reverently touched it to her mouth, following the glistening pattern of juice to her chin. With a curt nod, he released the napkin to the right of her platter and returned to his seat.

"Forgive me if I seem forward." His lush accent drifted across the table as she tried once more to place it; it seemed to be from everywhere and nowhere at once. "It would be a terrible shame if you sullied the fine ensemble you chose to wear this evening as my dinner companion."

She knew he was baiting her, yet his remark made her well aware of the clothing choice she made nonetheless.

"I'm sorry to disappoint you, Solaus." She smiled sweetly. "I came to perform a business service. I wasn't aware that dinner parties were a requirement."

His passionate, blue eyes raked her tank top-clad figure over very slowly as if he savored the vision of her far more than the food set before him. Kaitlin suddenly wished she'd donned something a bit more ravishing.

Sol's eyes twinkled with unspoken emotion. "I have no doubt, Miss Sommers, you are as lovely in any state of dress or disarray that I could … imagine."

He hesitated slightly before he spoke the last word and her head began to spin visions of his lips on hers.

"I'm afraid perhaps I've had a little too much wine."

Solaus didn't counter her remark, but raised a quizzical brow at the nearly full bottle by her side.

"Mark'het made me aware of the situation you encountered on your voyage to the island," he began tentatively. "It could be that you are merely tired and still a little ill after your experience."

Those last words escaped his throat with such a force that she was instantly shocked out of her reverie and caught a glimpse of possessive fury.

They all must know what happened she thought to herself, and of course Mark'het had been right to tell them. They all needed to be very aware of the danger that lurked, waiting for her or anyone to give an indication of the whereabouts of the treasure.

Whose side am I on, now? she asked herself, a clear picture of Nigel coming to the forefront of her vision. That picture wavered in view of Sol's darkly handsome face and then disappeared entirely when he spoke once more.

"Will you allow me to escort you to your room?" he asked, and this time concern rang true in his tone. Kaitlin nodded and he rose instantly, crossing the distance in a mere few short strides with his lean, long legs.

He offered her his arm in the most archaic and proper manner, and when she didn't respond immediately to his gesture, he mistook her mesmerized stare at his graceful crossing for an issue of propriety.

"I promise you will be quite safe with me, Kaitlin." He spoke her name as if it were a gift to words.

"I wonder in which time period you were born," she said

softly as she rose to meet his antiquated offering, and placed her hand upon his silk-covered arm. Though the fabric was cool to the touch, his flesh burned beneath and she could nearly taste his skin once more at just the thought of it.

"If I may be so bold as to trust your confidence, I shall explain a little of myself to you," Sol said as he navigated the cold stone corridors of his domain with Kaitlin in one hand and an electric lantern in the other.

"I prefer firelight," she said as the bright, white glare of the unnatural light swung wide and hit her eyes.

"As do I." He laughed and she could feel his muscles relaxing beneath her fingertips. "Though I cannot tell you why. In truth, I do not remember anything of myself before Drosk and his group discovered me in the underwater cavern."

"Did he save your life?" she asked, unable to restrain her inquiry.

"That is a tale I will leave for him to tell," he said cryptically as their footsteps echoed on the flagstones of the empty corridor.

She was deeply disappointed when they reached her room so quickly, but he dispelled that by gently taking her shoulders in both hands and turning her to face him in the eerie light.

"I mean to say to you that I know everything—and nothing."

His sad smile wounded her heart.

He continued. "I know all that happens around me. I am aware of world events. I have the knowledge of the world past and that of the leaders who stand before me today, but I do not know who I am."

"You are Solaus," she offered him as much as she could.

"I am Solaus because I was so named by a sailor who found me on the expedition. Solaus is Latin for 'alone' and alone, I surely am."

She wanted to reach out to him, to touch him and share with him her warmth, but he had already backed away from their encounter.

Removed those few short spaces from her, he reached through lantern light and darkness and took her hand in an exaggerated motion. His movements were not unlike the boy who shyly gave his affections to her before dinner.

"Until we meet again." His words echoed that of the child and reached her from the darkness as her senses registered his lips on the back of her hand.

"I'll bet you waited all night to do that," she whispered into the night air, completely alone in the dark hall.

Chapter Six

There was no moon in the midnight sky that night, so he had only starlight to guide his restless footsteps, not that any direction was needed. He'd paced up and down the dock so many times that evening that he was aware of every creaking board along the weathered planks.

Sleep had eluded Lucien for many hours already, but he felt more alert and awake than he could ever remember. The shanty town changed dramatically as the day wore on, and he took notice as the makeshift port went from a supply business in the daylight to an unruly town full of tavern brawls and any number of sins one could desire—for a price.

Lucien couldn't have what he desired, however. What he desired had slipped through a hole in the floor of the shack he occupied during his necessary visits to the smuggler's haven.

At first he was impressed by her obvious strength and character. He had even looked fondly forward to a challenging game of cat and mouse with her on the dangerous island. When it became apparent she was no longer on the playing field, he flew into a fit of rage that he was barley able to control. His last remaining helper climbed down into the hole at the charismatic madman's bidding to search her out. That had made it far easier to dispose of his body as well.

He slowed his pace once more as he reached the then empty

shack. His partner wouldn't be happy to discover he had to replace two of their associates.

"You won't be Nigel's girl for much longer," he whispered into the darkness, and leaned almost casually against the rickety frame of the dilapidated hut.

Two doors down, a much larger building rattled with the sounds of music and laughter. He turned his head slightly as the door to the impressive structure creaked open, spilling warm, inviting light onto the cold, bleached wood of the pier.

The air around him was instantly filled with the aroma of liquors, exotic smoke and perfume. This fanfare for the senses heralded the exit of a group of women, and judging by their dress and behavior, their reputations were probably as slender as their scantily clad figures.

He cared very little if they noticed him or not. His appetites this night ran far deeper than any of these ladies could fulfill. At the very least, he was weary of trying to come up with new ways to jettison all these bodies. He'd hate to have to do it once more if things turned sour during their business transaction.

As if on cue, they turned as one to regard him as a potential customer. One dark-haired girl approached him, her chest puffed out, feeling quite safe with her friends at her back, he imagined.

"Cold evening to be standing out here, alone," she needlessly pointed out. Her group edged closer to stare at him with interest. Slowly, she looked him up and down, measuring his ability to pay, or perhaps trying to make out his character.

"Good Evening to you, Madam," he addressed her formally. "I do enjoy my evenings alone, you are quite right."

It was impossible to mistake the disinterest in his tone, and the lead girl turned away unwilling to waste any more of her time in the chilly evening air. As they trailed off, something caught his eye and he slipped quietly up behind the unaware group of women.

"Excuse me," he said softly as he laid one hand on the shoulder of a timid looking girl in the back. Startled, she jumped and spun around, her voluminous hair falling out of her black velvet hat. It cascaded in gold ringlets down her shoulders and she giggled nervously. The others grumbled when they saw he had singled her out and walked on, leaving her alone with the dark stranger.

"Tell me," he asked in an even tone as he pulled a large amount of money from his pocket, "do you like to play games?"

Her eyes grew wide and she nodded wordlessly. He gave her one last approving glance, then ushered her to the shanty where he knew they wouldn't be disturbed. Once inside, he motioned for her to take a seat in the chair previously occupied by his lost captive.

She gingerly stepped around the jagged hole in the middle of the floorboards, and though she gave him a puzzled look as she passed, she knew well enough not to ask any questions of the patrons who frequented this island.

Kneeling beside her, he took her face gently in his hands and gazed into her blue eyes with all the passion and wonder one soul could hold for another person. She gasped at the ardent nature of his stare and a brief look of panic crossed her features as she recognized the face of madness.

"Tell me you love me, Dove," he whispered as his lips caressed her cheek.

"I love you." Trembling and afraid to do anything to arouse his ire, she answered him simply and quickly.

"Good girl." His breath was hot and rapid against her skin. "Do exactly as I tell you and I promise you will not get hurt—"

She nodded, afraid to try to find her voice a second time.

"—very much," he added.

•

Despite the fact that Kaitlin had tightly closed the shutters over the small window in her quarters, the sun insistently penetrated the wooden cracks wherever it could to let her know the next day had arrived.

The iron bars on the window itself didn't disturb her entirely, as she was able to reach right through them to open and close the functional shutters. None of the windows in this place seemed to employ any glass. She did wonder if the bars were meant to keep out intruders as they implied, or to keep her in.

The fire in the grate across the room had died to embers in the night. She was thankful for that bright orange glow in the center of the white ash; it would certainly make the morning fire easy to start.

The stone floor was nearly covered with a colorful array of plush oriental carpets in a dizzying collection of designs. As she sat up in the polished mahogany four-poster bed, she realized her bare feet wouldn't encounter any part of the cool stone floor if she walked over to the fireplace.

Renegade sunlight streamed in slanted rays across the room, and as Kaitlin crossed the distance, she felt the warm spots where it had fallen and the carpets had soaked it in for a time.

The fireplace was a smaller version of the one in the dining hall, designed so the rock would hold the fire's heat and keep the room as warm as possible as it gradually burned down throughout the night.

Her chamber looked like it had been transported out of an ancient European castle, made almost entirely of limestone commonly found in the West. There was very little wood present in the makeup of the structure, which she found surprising at first, though it made sense.

Kaitlin smiled as she looked around her quarters. Whatever the room lacked in modern comforts, the exotic and eclectic furnishings inside made up for it. There was a wash area in a small alcove off to the side, and it looked as if a recently installed lavatory and porcelain bath were going to make her stay much more pleasant.

She ran hot water into the basin in front of the mirror and then mixed the cold from the adjacent faucet until it became a comfortable temperature. At that moment, the steaming cloth on her face felt more luxurious than any expensive spa treatment she could remember having.

An underlying excitement ran through her veins, a nervous feeling in the pit of her stomach, and she realized she'd been thinking of Solaus as she dressed and made herself ready.

"You're acting like a teenager on a date." She laughed to herself but couldn't shake the feeling. She felt more alive than she ever had and welcomed this new chance to experience these feelings.

With a quick glance around the room to make sure her door was securely closed, she walked over to the bed and knelt down on the floor next to it. The carpets were thick and comfortable, cushioning her knees as she slid one arm between the mattresses. The hard outline of the medallion made contact with her fingers and she felt a moment of relief.

"Should you be keeping this from everyone now that you're here?" she asked herself. When she could come up with no clear answer, her fingers released her grip on the artifact and left it in the secret place. "Just for now because I couldn't possibly explain it," she said assuredly to no one in particular.

A small knock on the door brought her back around and she took a good look at herself sitting on the floor and talking to furnishings. She quickly stood and began to pull the disheveled blankets into place, hoping to give no one cause to come in and tuck anything somewhere she wouldn't want them to.

"Come in," she called as nonchalantly as possible.

The heavy door swung inward and she saw the top of Develin's head assert itself into the opening. Though his hair was dark, his skin was unusually fair, and that fairness was even more marked by the blush on his cheeks.

"Mother sent me for you. It is breakfast time now."

He flashed his excited grin as he regarded the outline of her figure in her shamefully sheer summer dress. The cream-colored gauze clung to her shapely legs and hips, and she had visions of herself standing in the face of a sultry ocean breeze, dangerously close to the rocks as Solaus watched her secretly from a barred window high along the western wall.

With her own cheeks colored by her romantic fantasy, she came forward and took the boy's hand. The smile remained on his face, which he shyly cast down at his sandals as they went forward.

She thought she knew the way to the dining hall and was a little surprised when he led her around the corridor and down half a flight of stone stairs she hadn't encountered the evening before.

Though she was a little lost and confused by the maze of hallways, it wasn't a moment longer before her senses were overwhelmed by the smell of bacon and eggs and fresh-baked bread. A comical thought came to mind and she remembered the cartoons she watched as a girl, of the characters who floated into the air and followed the aroma ribbons of food with their little feet flapping away.

After her near miss with dinner the evening before and the pastry Mark'het had afforded her far gone, she felt like she could follow her nose to any section of the keep with total reliability.

Develin was also inspired and pulled her forward with a hungry urgency that could only be brought on by youth. She realized she was tightly grasping his small hand, though he didn't seem to notice. Her stomach fluttered again, this time a helpless pawn to her emotions, as thoughts of her dark-haired mystery man entered her mind.

She longed to see his face. Even with the turmoil in his eyes she loved to see her image reflected there. She felt he was truly seeing her. So often she walked through life being viewed for who she was on the surface, never for who she was inside.

"Perhaps we must be able to see ourselves for who we really are before anyone else can see past the outside," she murmured quietly to herself.

Kaitlin and the boy were in the kitchen before they'd gone ten yards down the corridor at the bottom of the stairs. All the work had been done and she wished she'd been called earlier to lend a hand to Develin's mother. She was definitely much the better after a full night's rest.

The kitchen was large and equipped with stainless steel sinks and counters. It almost resembled a cafeteria in the layout and she wondered what the facility had been used for in the past. Perhaps it had been a prison, but most likely it was utilized as it was being employed now—a safe house for those who didn't wish to be found.

Kaitlin fantasized about the rocky fortification. What notorious gangster had stayed here, what political refugee? She briefly considered the passionate rendezvous between secret lovers that might have happened at this secluded and secure depot.

Though the cookware in the nearby sink told a tale of fabulous dishes in the making, Kaitlin briefly wondered why Develin had led her into this empty room. He continued to propel her across the red tiles of the flooring and around a rack thick with silver pots and pans. She noticed a side door behind the shelving and followed him through that as well, knowing herself to be lost and at his mercy.

A cool, salty breeze flowed over her face as she stepped onto a stone terrace. The sun was rising to the east, though well on its way as it painted the sky with the remaining colors of a faded palette on the lingering dawn.

The first thing she noticed on the patio was the lush, planted palms and vibrantly green plant life crawling over most of the area. It truly seemed like a tropical oasis with bubbling waterfalls and brightly colored birds nesting in the branches of the potted trees.

The second thing that captured her attention was a stunningly beautiful woman seated at the table next to the elaborately carved stone railing that made up the edge of the balcony.

Her pale skin glowed like the moonlight, and clearly the sun was envious of the delicate hue because it didn't seem to fall there and compete with her radiance.

Kaitlin's heart sunk and she felt an irrational moment of jealousy at the presence of this green-eyed beauty, of the fact that Solaus must surely be her amour.

"Greetings, Kaitlin," she said with a refined English accent. She extended one exquisite arm with a perfect hand.

She noticed the woman's familiar use of her name and autopilot took over as she moved forward to stiffly grasp the hand offered. The lady didn't rise to greet her.

Before she could release her perfunctory shake, Develin ran forward and laid a kiss directly on the woman's cheek. Kaitlin thought she would fall apart with jealousy.

"How is breakfast, Mother?" he inquired before the woman in front of her noticed Kaitlin's stare.

"Your father has done us a great honor this morning, as always." She smiled with an honest joy that caused Kaitlin's heart to warm instantly.

"Ah, there you are!" Drosk's voice bellowed from behind as Develin took a seat by his mother, all the while casting her in an adoring stare.

With one hand supporting a silver platter laden with food, Drosk swept by her and in the same movement pulled a chair from the table with his free hand.

Kaitlin was awestruck by the fluidity of his motion and quite impressed at his gallantry as he seated her and laid the table out all in one minute. She'd be completely remiss if she didn't also notice the loving way Drosk attended to his wife.

"I apologize," the dark-haired beauty said as she was seated. The true distress on her face was noticeable. "I didn't mean to call you so familiarly, by your first name, without your permission."

"I hope you'll call me your friend." Kaitlin beamed and felt an instant connection with the woman across from her.

"Ah." Drosk nodded knowingly to all the general occupants of the table and Develin leaned back as if he was preparing to listen to a story he loved well. "You might wonder, Miss Kaitlin, why such a lovely lady would consent to be my wife?"

The experienced and worldly photojournalist was immediately reduced to a shy and precocious child, and she truly did harbor a desire to know what drew such a stunning woman to her exciting but nonetheless dangerous treasure-hunting acquaintance. The look of anticipation on her face was all it took to encourage him to continue.

"I believe it was in the new Library of Alexandria," he began, and instantly Develin rolled his eyes in his mother's direction.

"You were a wayward fool, looking for treasure," she added as if on cue, and actually paused for him to intercede.

"I was a respected archaeologist," he interjected, arching an eyebrow at her smug smile.

"I never could resist a man with a good heart," she answered. Her love for him shone in her eyes.

"And I could never resist an assistant curator of the Library of Alexandria," he finished with a flourish of his hands over the table.

The charming woman grew pensive before them as if considering all the assistant curators of that institution.

"I suppose Mrs. Dodson was right out," she said perfunctorily, looking at him.

"Hmm, yes," he agreed in an almost acceding tone. "Ms. Hardbough was a tough one as well."

"Oh?" Kaitlin inquired with polite interest, unable to resist the word play. "In what way?"

"In the way that she had thirty cats and her husband Bernice might thump me on the head?" Drosk responded as though that answer had been given a dozen times.

"Does it matter when a gentle woman's husband does not introduce her to such lovely company?" the woman said teasingly, but still with a tone of assertion.

"Miss Kaitlin, may I introduce you to my wife, Lilly,"

Develin jumped from his seat at the table, a look of horror on his face. "I am out of juice," the boy said with a laugh.

"Allow me, son." Drosk immediately stood and reached for the pitcher. With a small gesture, one that would be overlooked by many, Lilly reached forward and took the glass handle of the pitcher.

Develin gave her a closely guarded look, as did Drosk, when she lifted it from the table.

"I can certainly retrieve juice for our son," she said proudly to those present, and Kaitlin didn't doubt it for a moment. Her faithful feelings did nothing to ease the concern on Drosk's face, however.

The strong-willed woman sat the pitcher on her lap and much to Kaitlin's surprise, she proceeded to grip the wheels of her wheelchair and pull back from the table. It took a strong effort for her not to look at the surprise on Kaitlin's face as she wheeled past the breakfast companions and into the other room.

It was no wonder she didn't rise to greet her earlier, Kaitlin realized, and looked up to regard the mask of sorrow on Drosk's face.

"Lady," he said solemnly to his stunned guest as Lilly gracefully made her way into the kitchen. "We all have different reasons to search for treasure. Now you have seen mine."

A moment of painful memory flashed before Kaitlin's eyes at his solemn words and she saw the shadowy, dangerous face of her island captor for one instant.

"We may be here for the same thing," he had said in front of her so calmly, to the man who would shortly meet his death. "But we are not here for the same reason."

Kaitlin gripped the edge of the table, unwilling to give in to the swoon that so often left her reviewing another life. It took only a moment for her to compose herself, but in that moment Lilly was at her side.

"She will be fine," Lilly's gentle voice said over her head as cool white fingers stroked her hairline comfortingly.

"She will be fine when Solaus returns," a deep voice added knowingly.

"I believe, husband, perhaps this one time you may actually be correct." Her sweet voice offered no discontent.

Kaitlin took a deep breath and resolved to banish the terrifying image of her abductor from her thoughts. Deep inside she shivered at the idea he might still be searching for her, but she had to believe he was after the medallion. Not having found it, he surely must have turned elsewhere.

"I'm quite alright." She cast a brave smile at her companions, and with a hand that barely shook, ladled an assortment of exotic fruits onto her breakfast plate for a start. No one else at the table appeared to move and she really thought they might be holding their breath as she took her weighty fork and captured a sweet looking mango.

The plump, fleshy fruit released the most heavenly juices in her mouth and she savored them for quite a while with her eyes closed, basking in the warm sun. The moment she swallowed, Develin broke into a peal of delighted laughter while Drosk and Lilly attempted to refrain by hiding their smiles behind their hands. She realized they'd all watched her take her first bite, and she was a little curious.

"Now what did I do?" she asked with wide eyes, which caused

Develin to fall into another fit of delight.

"I apologize," Drosk said and elbowed his son next to him. "You see, Mark'het told us you will eat nothing but Pop Tarts. So he had us put one aside before he took Master Solaus to the shore this morning, with the instructions that we are only to give it to you if absolutely necessary."

"Well, is it apple cinnamon?"

"Solaus said we are not to tell you." Develin squirmed in his seat, grinning ear to ear.

"So then Solaus won't be joining us." She tried to keep the disappointment out of her voice as she realized her host was not at home, but did a poor job of it.

Lilly nodded to her with a look of empathy, but Kaitlin didn't miss Drosk's sly wink at the two across the table.

"That's good," she said in a bit of an exaggerated tone. "That will give me time to get my bearings and work on the equipment setup."

"And of course, we are all here to help you with what you need," the handsome Egyptian native reassured her. Kaitlin could easily see why Lilly would consent to marry this charming, generous man.

With a full stomach and the hot Mediterranean sun bathing her skin, she took a few minutes to gaze around the terrace. It all seemed very luxurious and peaceful, though an item near one edge of the platform kept catching her eye. Her vision wandered among the many exquisite objects in the little haven, but her mind kept coming back to the fixture and her curiosity piqued.

"I believe this really might be the strangest fountain I've ever seen," she commented aloud and rose to inspect it.

"That's because it's not a fountain," Lilly answered her with delight. She moved her chair to stand by Kaitlin and the odd looking item.

The bulk of the contraption was a large, stoneware bowl of

some type, which had a constant level of water inside fed to it from a source above in a reservoir. The water from the large bowl poured out in a steady stream into a cylindrical jar. This jar had some type of marker that floated inside and as the water rose, the marker slowly passed up several notches etched into the cylinder.

"This is a water clock," Lilly said in a tone that almost reminded her of a school teacher. She was clearly in her element then. "It is an example of one of the first time-calculating devices ever created. In ancient Alexandria, there was a famous inventor known as Ctesibius, who made this very design, we believe. Though none of his writing survived the burning of the Library of Alexandria by Roman conquerors, his work was mentioned and outlined by another famous inventor later on—Archimedes. Many versions were designed for many centuries after, but this one started it all. This must be the most authentic replica I have ever heard of in existence."

Lilly looked up at Kaitlin's fascinated expression as if to explain her passion. "Though I am bound in this wheelchair, my mind yet walks through the history of time."

"She seems to know quite a lot about these artifacts Sol keeps so close to his heart." Drosk smiled proudly at his wife who returned his gaze with fiery eyes.

"This is one of the items," Kaitlin exclaimed, and before she could ask what it was doing out on a balcony in plain sight, Lilly answered her.

"It was such an unusual occurrence," she began, her tone slightly puzzled after all this time. "When we unpacked the artifacts, I immediately knew what this could be but I had no idea how to set it up and how it functioned. Though Solaus has no memory of his past, he certainly did know how to put the clock together and had it running precisely in no time at all."

"I think he was as surprised as we were," Drosk interjected

a little uneasily. "Solaus must have been a great treasure hunter before he forgot."

"More likely a wise librarian," Lilly put in, glancing at her husband and smiling wryly.

"Yes, whatever you say, dear," he added by rote.

Develin looked to his mother next.

"Because I am right?" she inquired archly as her husband crossed the terrace to them.

"Perhaps, but because you are also beautiful," he conceded and gave her a gentle kiss on the cheek.

Kaitlin glanced over to their son who was making quite a face at the display. She felt a longing in her heart that caused her to think of her mysterious host, now away from the keep. She was more than afraid she'd have a lot of time by herself to think on how she felt about his absence now that she was here and subject to his whim.

"Do you know where I'll be setting up?" she asked a little abruptly, partially to ease the sweet ache in her heart at the sight of the happy couple, but mostly because she decided it was best to jump right in and start on the project. The busier she was, the less time she would have to dwell on her feelings for this seductive stranger who always seemed to occupy her thoughts.

"Develin and I will clean up here if you would like to take Miss Sommers to the display room?" Though Lilly framed the statement in the form of a question, there was clearly no other option in her tone.

"I would be delighted." Drosk sighed, but with a happy smile on his face. He looked briefly to his son who was still working on his meal. "You do as your mother says and help her finish here."

"I would be delighted," the boy answered wistfully, rolling his eyes in exaggeration.

Drosk began walking toward the door with Kaitlin at his side. "Kids that age, you know, are so impossible," he spoke rather loudly over his shoulder.

The laughter that trailed their footsteps through the kitchen told her Develin had heard every word, as intended.

•

The area that Drosk led her to was spacious and cool. The afternoon sun glowed through the glass in the windows, the first real pane she'd seen since she'd been here. Beneath her feet, the stone had been covered in a muted, blonde hardwood flooring.

"We have climate controls in this room to keep it at an even temperature at all times while we work on the cataloging of the objects."

He motioned to a panel on the wall that was already running a comfortable program. Kaitlin nodded her understanding as she began to get a feel for the lighting and atmosphere.

There were different types of furnishings in the room, tables and chairs, but nothing elaborate as they were there to serve a function and not impress.

She wandered through the area and came to a small table covered with magazines. It didn't take long for her to realize they belonged to her publication, nor for her to see her very own photographs on the covers.

"What is this?" she asked, truly puzzled by the appearance of her art on the coffee table.

"Oh, yes," her guide answered with a smile. "Solaus was very wary, as you might understand, to bring anyone to this location."

"Of course," she responded automatically, her cheeks coloring at the thought of her deception.

"When your name was suggested by an associate, he was a bit uncertain because this was a man we did not entirely trust. When he saw your work, he was deeply moved. He said he knew by your photographs that you saw the soul behind the story, the truth behind the history."

Kaitlin was stunned and too ashamed to take the compliment

under the pretenses in which she came. She felt much more like a pawn in a game she didn't wish to play than a visionary who deserved accolades. To take the attention from her flushed appearance, she stood and crossed the room to lay her hands on an intricately carved maple wardrobe leaning against the far wall.

"Is this where you keep the bodies of all the previous photographers?" she asked in an attempt to change the subject.

"Only the ones who did not perform to the best of their abilities, of course," he answered, leaning against the wall next to the wooden frame. "I will tell you a secret, though. This is a door. And behind it is a treasure that would surely rival the contents of Aladdin's cave."

"Are there any magic lamps inside that will grant me wishes?" she joked half-heartedly and Drosk regarded her with a sad smile.

"Not that I have found thus far, Miss Kaitlin." He held a look of hope in his eyes and Kaitlin knew it was for Lilly. "Though occasionally I do wonder. The things that go on here sometimes are—unusual to say the least."

"Then I ought to feel perfectly comfortable here," she added wryly, thinking of all the strange visions and feelings she'd experienced since coming to Cairo.

"Solaus has the key," he informed her. "We do not usually go in the room without him unless we are picking out your dinnerware."

Kaitlin's eyes grew wide and she had to ask, "So that cup I drank from last evening really could be the Holy Grail?"

He shrugged but seemed to enjoy her excitement. It would be difficult for everyone involved not to be thrilled by the prospect of the new discovery before them.

"My wife has been a great asset to Solaus. Her knowledge of the history of the Mediterranean culture was very useful as he began the cataloging. It is a strange thing that Sol can do. He seems to know intimate details about most of the objects with the find, knows what their purposes are but nothing of the history behind the item."

"He seems like a very mysterious man," she said nonchalantly over her shoulder as they opened the equipment cases.

"Indeed," Drosk conceded. "How can he be anything else when he knows so very little of himself as it is? The only things he can be sure of are his passions—the only lead he can follow at this time."

She stopped setting up to regard her assistant thoughtfully. "I wonder if that's why he distances himself emotionally, because that's all he has."

"Does he do that?" Drosk smirked, turning to face her openly.

She abruptly put her back to him feigning disinterest. Though she successfully hid her expression from him, she couldn't possibly miss his knowing chuckle.

The afternoon flew by swiftly, but with Drosk's assistance, she was able to get the studio up and running by late afternoon. Just as they laid out the filters and got the light meters ready, Lilly and Develin came in to inspect their handiwork.

"It looks like we are in business." Lilly nodded with delight. There was an air of expectation in the room and each person felt inside as if they were on the verge of something electric, something exciting—something that would change their lives forever.

"I know you must be weary, going straight to work after your journey here," Lilly said kindly. "I have something for you. Develin will fetch it for me and then I think you should rest a while, explore the stronghold and make yourself at home until dinner is ready."

The prospect of exploring the keep did appeal to her a great deal and she found herself eager to stretch her legs and have a little freedom for a while.

"I'd like that," she said just as Develin came in from the outside corridor holding a box, which he extended to her.

She took it, and probably from lifting equipment cases all day, fully expected it to be heavy. It was very light, and she pulled off the top to find a stunningly smooth, white satin slip dress inside.

The cool fabric unfolded with a soft grace as she wrapped her fingers around the straps of the gown and held it out. The simplicity of the design made it purely elegant and she could hardly remember ever being in such awe of a garment before.

"This is so lovely, Lilly," she began, deeply touched by the gift.

"It really is nothing." The dark-haired woman smiled. "Solaus had mentioned to me early this morning that you had nothing to wear to dinner, and I had so many things that I've never tried on. It's better for the dress to find a home with someone who will wear it."

"Then I'll see you this evening and be very honored to wear this dress."

"I do not believe you will be seeing us tonight." Drosk coughed slightly. "Solaus has requested your company at dinner alone once again. Apparently, he did not get enough of you last evening."

"Drosk!" Lilly exclaimed, reaching out a slender arm and smacking him gently on the rump.

"I like that, you know." He winked at her and a slight hue of red passed across her delicate features.

"With your permission we will leave you to your own devices for the rest of the afternoon. Drosk will come for you when he has prepared dinner." Lilly seemed satisfied by Kaitlin's nod and turned to her son.

"Develin, please take Miss Sommers' box to her room and set it on the bed. The moment you're finished, return to our apartments and begin the school work I've left on the table for you."

He was still young enough to pout and Kaitlin had no doubt he'd be dragging his feet the entire way. She imagined it would give Drosk and Lilly some time to spend together.

"That sounds good to me," she agreed, and patted him on the head as he huffed across the room with her package.

She started on the terrace, still fascinated by the ancient water clock. Kaitlin carried her favorite 35 mm camera, strap dangling from her wrist as she began to see her surroundings with an artist's eye—an ability she'd long possessed. The state of her perception always felt as if she had fallen back a step inside herself. Strange how that feeling of falling inward could allow her to see more expansively outside than a normal glance at her environment.

The sun was beginning its descent into the evening sky, though it had yet to color the clouds gathering overhead. As she focused on the unusual clock, she could almost hear the sound of sandals crossing a sand swept plaza, feel the excitement of the citizens of Alexandria all those years ago. Seeing something from that time period made her feel a deep connection to the past and those who inhabited it.

She took several photographs of the priceless relic that Solaus had so generously allowed Lilly to keep in her little oasis before she began to wonder how easily this patio could be accessed from the outside. With a few shorts steps, she walked to the edge and leaned over.

The terrace was up along the northern wall of the stronghold far enough that she didn't believe it would be possible for anyone to reach it—not that a person could safely anchor anywhere near the treacherous, jutting rocks that surrounded the base of the structure.

She noticed a flat spot nestled in a part of the outcropping, not overly large but perhaps a comfortable place for her to stand and be near the water. The spot was far below and she considered that there might be some type of cellar access leading out onto the rocks.

Excited at the prospect of discovering a hidden door, Kaitlin found her way back to her room easily with the intention of putting the expensive camera on a shelf before she adventured into slippery territory.

As soon as she was near enough to her chamber to see the door, she realized it was slightly ajar. Her heartbeat rapidly increased and she felt a moment of anxiety as she drew closer to determine if she could discern any noise from inside.

"You're being foolish," she told herself firmly. "This is a safe location, only one way into the keep and it's locked at all times. More than likely, Develin left it open."

A true moment of panic gripped her as she remembered his light rap on the door this morning as she was secretly checking on the amulet. How long had he been there, too shy perhaps to say anything at first?

With nothing but concern on the forefront of her mind, she pushed the door open and strode boldly to the center of the room. Develin sat cross-legged next to the bed, and in his small hands the amulet radiated a warm glow.

Kaitlin gasped at the sight and immediately rushed to the boy who didn't notice her entrance.

"Develin," she said softly, trying to imagine the best way to release him from the alluring grasp of the artifact.

Gently, she covered his hands with her own, effectively breaking his visual contact with the medallion. Though the skin on the back of his hands felt warm, it didn't seem dangerously so and she breathed a deep sigh of relief. At that sound, he looked up into her eyes as if he'd just awakened from a dream.

"I didn't mean to look at it." He sounded so contrite it broke Kaitlin's heart to hear his distress. "It's just that I saw you earlier. I thought there might be a magic treasure hidden away and I just had to see."

The relieved woman considered his heritage and thought it was no wonder the child had a natural curiosity for things like this. With a light pull, she released his fingers and drew it away from him.

"If the truth must be told, Develin," she said to the boy in confidential tones, "I'm amazed by this object as well."

"Is it magic?" he asked, eyes wide with hope and wonder, and she couldn't do anything to dash his dreams.

"I believe it very well may be but until we know more about my necklace, we should probably keep it safe."

He had an extremely pensive look on his young face and she scrambled for a way in her mind to convince him to keep her secret. Fortunately, the boy and his imagination did all the work for her.

"If I make a wish with it, will it come true?" he inquired a little nervously as if the answer might change his idea about the way the world worked.

"Wishes are magic, if you have three." The little girl inside her found that familiar chant once again and she unintentionally said it so easily that his face lit up with belief.

"Please." He held out his hands in awe. "May I have one of the wishes?"

Looking into his teary eyes and seeing the hope and love there, Kaitlin couldn't deny him his wish even if she had to pretend. With a reverent grace, she laid the medallion in the palm of his hands and watched as he squeezed his eyes tight.

The room instantly grew warmer and she felt a little disoriented, kneeling as she was in front of the boy. There was no fire in the fireplace yet she could hear crackling flames all around her. There was a pull deep inside her, a passionate longing that compelled her to close her eyes and dream of impossible things.

As soon as the heat wave passed over them, she opened her eyes and saw Develin hold the amulet out to her.

"Did you make your wish?" She asked him carefully. When he nodded, she was relieved. "Remember, you must not tell anyone about the wish or my necklace. If you do, it may not come true."

She truly felt uneasy, creating a myth like that to encourage his silence, but she wasn't ready for the medallion to be revealed.

Besides, she told herself to ease her conscience, *it's always said if you tell someone your wish, it won't come to pass. For all I know, it's completely proper advice.*

"Perhaps there's something you can help me with now," she began. "I noticed a little spot out on the rocks down below. Would you happen to know if there's a door or window near so I can go out there?"

"Boy would I!" He jumped to his feet, the adventure of the medallion replaced by a new intrigue. "I can show you, but you must promise not to tell anyone. Mother says it's very dangerous out on the rocks and I'm not supposed to know about things like special doors."

"I'll never tell."

She smiled and pointedly tucked the medallion between the mattresses once again. Perhaps she'd find a new place for it later, but there was no sense in tempting Develin to look for it once again if he thought it would always be there. After all, half the fun of finding treasure was looking for it.

•

There wasn't much of a cellar below the building, and she imagined the Mediterranean would have something to say about it if anyone ever did try to construct one.

Develin bid her farewell among the antique wine racks, casks and bottles of beer. From the look of things, some of those spirits had been hanging around the racks for far longer than the lively occupants of the building.

The outside door was wooden and very narrow, painted the color of the stone that made up the walls in the small room. The door was barely noticeable, half hidden behind a dusty set of shelves. The bolt attaching it to the frame was slightly rusty, but she was quite sure her little guide had been through it at least once so she knew it would open.

With nimble fingers, Kaitlin unlocked the door and pushed the groaning planks outward. Though it only gave a few inches with her initial thrust, she was immediately struck by the damp, salty air that engulfed her in a strong breeze. She opened the door well enough to squeeze through and held her breath as she pushed it closed behind.

She found herself in a small, narrow stone passage, perhaps only half a dozen yards long. The colorful twilight sky hung like a masterpiece in the stone frame of the roughly hewn exit up ahead. She ran her fingers along the rock wall as she walked, and noticed almost absently that the limestone became wet and slippery beneath her fingertips.

She was thrilled to be so near the ocean as she emerged from the passage, and went to the edge. The sunset was breathtaking and there was a gathering of darker clouds on the horizon. The salty spray smacked against the base of the rocks with intense force, gushing into the air high above her in a sparkling show before it cascaded down once more.

She was entranced by the dance of the spray, and watched it so intently she didn't notice the passing of time or the fast-moving storm front that had seemed like a harmless gathering of clouds just a while ago.

The sun finally said its farewell and dipped below the far horizon. With the absence of its warming light, she realized it had rapidly grown cold and the sparkling show was over. The suddenly insistent wind whipped her hair frantically, and she had a difficult time keeping it out of her eyes as the spray became a menacing wave that encroached upon the top of her rock with a threatening slap at her bare feet.

She was slightly alarmed and bent down to feel for the sandals she had so casually removed earlier. With one hand holding back her hair and the other feeling for her shoes she was knocked off balance when the next vicious wave hit the break.

It was almost totally dark, and she scrambled backwards as fast as she could across the slippery rock in the direction of the cave. A deep, heavy thunder rolled in the distance, announcing the intentions of the incoming tempest as the next wave hit.

Kaitlin issued a small cry of protest. The wave captured her helpless form and raked her along the rocky surface as it tried to pull her back into the sea. As she slipped away, she thought she saw a pale light through her stinging, water-drenched eyes and flung an arm out in that direction.

Strong arms grabbed her wrist first, then her shoulders as she was lifted out of danger. Her sheer summer dress was soaked completely through and torn in too many places. In her delirium, she tried to cover herself as her rescuer held her closely in his arms and made his way into the cellar.

Solaus laid her gently onto a roughly woven carpet in the small space inside. He lifted the lamp high to see if she had any immediate, serious injuries, but his hands were shaking and he was forced to set the light on the floor next to her, casting her in a half shadow.

As determined as he was to discern the seriousness of her cuts and bruises, his eyes were drawn to the wet, gauzy dress that clung to her. He delicately stroked the skin of her face. He was shocked to discover it was ice cold, and panicked.

"Please, be alright."

He breathed urgently as he slid next to her on the floor, pressing his hot frame against her cold, wet figure. Her eyes were closed, her lips nearly blue, but she responded to the warmth of his skin and turned slightly to press against him.

Solaus released a primal moan of desire as her curves conformed to his body, pushing against his mounting need. His strong, muscular arms wrapped around her, cradling her head in one hand as he held his cheek against hers.

His other hand firmly pressed her lower back to him. Though he desperately tried to be gentle, his prolonged defense against his passion for this beauty laying next to him had driven him to distraction for longer than she could know. He didn't think he could control his reaction to her response at his embrace.

He felt her lips turn against his cheek. The touch of her silky soft mouth sent shivers of agony and ecstasy up his spine. Her skin felt warm then, and with very little restraint left he turned his head to look at her.

"Solaus," she whispered, but sounded far away.

When she said his name, he pulled her close without realizing it and covered her lips with his own. He needed to taste her, and kissed her with a hunger that had haunted him for what seemed an eternity. She returned his attention with an urgent frenzy, her lips and tongue playing across his skin as if she couldn't be satisfied.

He moved the hand that held her head so carefully down her neck, between her shoulder blades, and pressed inward on her spine as she arched her back.

Her skin felt hot and sticky to the touch, and a moment of concern held back his ardor. He raised his hand behind her head once more and saw with confusion that it was covered in blood. Gently, he worked his fingers through her hair and she smiled, her eyes still closed, almost as if she were dreaming.

Solaus froze the moment he felt the swelling gash on the back of her head and released his passionate hold on her at once. With a clear head, he could see she was wounded and barely lucid.

Berating himself for nearly taking advantage of Kaitlin and possibly causing her more injury, he bent and lifted her as if she weighed nothing, determined to take her to safety even if it kept her from him.

Her eyelids fluttered open as he ascended the stairwell and entered the side hall in the main part of the building.

"What happened?" She looked into his eyes, genuinely confused but not a bit put out to be in his arms.

Drosk and Mark'het approached at a run when they saw him coming down the corridor, the concern on their faces turning to horror as they saw the blood on her dress and in her hair.

"Did you stoke the fire in her room?" he demanded brusquely, his emotions and desire still coloring his words. He strode on before they could answer, looking back at their stunned features over his shoulder before he added, "Fetch Lilly."

"Lilly is already waiting," Drosk called after him as he hurried toward the east wing of the fortress.

•

The fire in her guest room burned brightly, but did nothing to ward off the chill of the fever that blazed across Kaitlin's cheeks.

Lilly sat next to her bed in the event she might wake, but she slipped in and out of consciousness too randomly to hold an intelligent conversation with anyone. Everyone in the house was present except Develin who was sent to another part of the building on an errand because he worried himself so much over Kaitlin.

Solaus paced back and forth across the foot of the bed, his face strained as he cast worried glances in Kaitlin's direction every few seconds.

"She says your name very often," Lilly commented and reached for her hand as Kaitlin tossed and turned. "She must see a doctor, but she cannot be moved. You need to decide what we're going to do, Solaus."

"There is no question of whether or not we will bring a doctor here. If I have to walk to the end of the earth and carry one all the way to this room on my back, I will do so." Solaus stopped pacing and asked, "Who can we trust? Who will have her best interests at heart?"

"I think I know how to help," Mark'het said a little apprehensively.

"You know someone who could help?" Solaus asked abruptly, turning his way with overpowering intensity.

"I know who Kaitlin trusts; she told me," he said. "He will know what we need to do."

Chapter Seven

"What are we going to do?" Hestor exclaimed, wringing his hands with worry as he walked the length of the hotel lobby where Kaitlin's rooms were.

Fortunately by the time he arrived in Cairo, Mark'het had been able to remember most of the little things Kaitlin had mentioned to him about her dear friend, and after hitting up a few of Drosk's more reliable associates in the field, he got a number to call. Before he could even begin to explain the situation over the phone, the ancient historian was out the door and on his way to meet the captain.

"We just need a few quiet moments to think." Mark'het laid a hand on the wiry fellow's arm and calmed him a little.

"Do you know anyone here with a medical background? One who would come with me to see her?"

"There is a doctor across the street." Realization dawned on Hestor's face. "And he has taken care of her in the past."

"Then I may safely take him to her without fear he will speak of it to others?" Drosk asked, and looked to Hestor's expression for confirmation.

"I certainly do not see why this wouldn't work," Hestor said brightly, lifting his chin with pride. "It is a good thing you came to see me, you know. I have everything under control."

"Kaitlin was right to put her trust in you," the fishing boat captain made a grand show of patting the diminutive scholar on the back. "I'll go now to see this doctor and arrange for his travel."

Hestor instantly stopped beaming and narrowed his eyes suspiciously.

"You don't think you can go over there and talk to him without me. You need me to make the introduction because he does not know you." Hestor circled around to come between the exit and the Mark'het. "And, he knows me. I'd like to think he even trusts me to do the right thing for our girl."

Mark'het sighed but was unable to find anything but affection for the old man. A part of him knew if he let him come to the office, he'd have to let him go a lot further, but after knowing Kaitlin for such a short time he could understand how any friend of hers would worry.

"Yes, by all means come along, friend of Kaitlin." Mark'het laughed and motioned for him to lead the way.

The office seemed deserted, though the door was unlocked. They were the only people in the waiting room.

"Sit here just one moment." Hestor patted him grandly on the back with a big smile. "I will go and see if he is in."

Mark'het suppressed a grin as Hestor imitated the earlier patronizing clap on his back perfectly and knew the man was as sharp as a tack. With a nod, Hestor slipped down the dark hall toward Dr. Hollinger's office.

Mark'het decided it was lucky he had time to consider a way to give the little guy the slip before he flew back to Alexandria with the physician. He played out several scenarios in his mind, but could imagine nothing short of tying him up would let them get away unhindered—and even that was seriously doubtful.

Half an hour passed before Mark'het realized, as absorbed as he was with focusing on the imaginary getaway. After a glance at the clock on the wall, he was on his feet and about to go down the darkened hallway when he heard Hestor's voice coming toward him. He had no idea what the old man had told the medic, but he was more than afraid he'd been declined before they were even introduced.

When Hestor emerged with the doctor in tow, Mark'het breathed a sigh of relief and tried to discern the man's reaction to the situation by the look on his face. He was surprised to see the elderly physician didn't seem the least bit astonished by Hestor's story, and might even have looked mildly amused.

"I want to tell you right up front that I do not normally make secret house calls to strange places late in the night." Doctor Hollinger held up a hand to halt the outburst that was brimming on Mark'het's tongue. "However, I am particularly fond of this patient and am inclined to make an exception just this once."

"Oh, thank you." Mark'het breathed in relief. "We are so worried right now and—"

"On one condition," he added firmly, and crossed his arms over his white coat. The relieved fisherman glanced suspiciously at Hestor whose face was a mask of ignorance.

"Due to the circumstances of this situation, I have decided that it is in my best interest that Hestor accompany us to guarantee my safety." The doctor settled an obvious look on the scholar, as if to make certain he'd said it properly.

"Oh, really," Hestor said with feigned surprise. "Are you sure? I would not wish to be any trouble. Just let me get my things."

"If it were up to me, I would be delighted to have him along," Mark'het began, considering how many ways Solaus would skin him alive for bringing an additional person to the island.

"Listen carefully," Dr. Hollinger asserted before he could continue his thought. "Kaitlin's condition sounds very bad. If I am right—"

"He's always right," Hestor piped in from somewhere on the sidelines.

"If I am right," the doctor continued in a tone that let everyone know he would brook no more interruption, "we do not have a lot of time as it is. I can pretty much tell you that if we have to travel any distance at all to get to her, we will be wasting valuable minutes she might need by standing here arguing."

Mark'het knew this was a losing battle and had to weigh his decision carefully. He was very fond of Kaitlin, but there was the safety of other people to consider as well—like his brother and his brother's wife.

"I cannot pick and chose between friends," Mark'het eventually said. "I will just have to hope we can all trust you two and continue on."

"Good." Dr. Hollinger nodded. "I have a bag packed in my office at all times in the event of an emergency. Let me grab that and lock the building up behind us."

•

The trio of unlikely partners was so focused as they entered the street, that they missed the dim outline of a man lingering inside the twilight shadows right next to the doorway they exited. Those shadows had grown quite long from the time he followed Mark'het into the office, affording him almost total cover.

"Finally," Lucien said as he watched them walk away into the distance.

Slowly, he reached into his jacket pocket, holding his breath as he removed an unmarked envelope. With graceful movements, he reached inside the flap and slid one photograph out apart from the many inside.

The way he cradled the photo in the palm of his left hand was reverently tender, and he extended the fingertips of his free hand to lightly stroke the glossy surface of the picture. His breath became rapid as his fingers outlined the form of Kaitlin standing on a balcony in Nigel's arms.

"It will not be much longer, Dove," he whispered in a breathless tone as he began to walk across the Kahn to the meeting place his partner had designated earlier in the day. "And when that time comes, I will be certain you have no one to turn to but me."

It was fully dark over the streets of Cairo, but the bazaar was alight and alive with countless vendors and colorfully lit items to tempt the eye.

Lucien slipped among the crowds like a shadow, swiftly and with purpose as he came to a table at the very same café Hestor had said goodbye to Kaitlin.

He smiled as he saw the deep red bottle of Merlot on the table, and knew his associate was nearby. Taking an easy seat, his back to the wall, he said nothing as Panos approached and sat in the chair opposite. He seemed very uncomfortable in that position, something that made Lucien feel just a little better inside.

"The fishing boat captain met with Hestor today," Lucien stated casually as he poured two glasses of the dark red wine. With a swift look, Lucien couldn't discover any reaction on his accomplice's face and silently cursed the sunglasses the big man wore day and night. "If you are not careful, Nigel may not need you at all in a very short while. Then where would we be?" Lucien raised his glass to his partner and by habit, Panos lifted his.

Lucien was pleased to see the slight shake in Panos' hands, the telltale whitening of the skin around his fingers as he gripped the stem of the crystal a bit too forcefully. Lucien carefully set his goblet on the white linen tablecloth and removed the envelope. With a fast and fluid motion, he sealed it beyond any tampering and tossed it onto the table.

"When the time is right, slip this envelope into the mail the fisherman fetches for Solaus whenever he comes for supplies." He couldn't help but smile at the thought of the outcome.

"What is it?" Panos asked warily.

"Something that will solve your problem and mine all in one go." He answered simply, as if it could be nothing less than that.

"We have different problems?" Panos had to ask, crossing his big arms across his chest.

"Oh, you have no idea, my friend. You really don't," Lucien stated flatly, his mind filling with visions of Kaitlin strapped to the chair and helpless against him. But she'd told him her secret. His heart beat fast at the memory of the moment she'd reached out to him and bared her soul with such beauty and strength.

"Just for me," he whispered under his breath, caught up in the recollection.

"I'm sorry?" Panos interrupted, clearly annoyed by the behavior, and destroying the passionate fantasy Lucien was building in his mind.

"Just do as I say." Lucien's voice was like ice and cut through the myriad of sounds that flooded the marketplace. Without another word, he picked up the bottle of wine and disappeared into the crowd.

•

Kaitlin's head felt as if it was stuffed with cotton. Her eyes didn't want to open. For a brief moment she attempted to recall just how much she'd been drinking the night before and what it was, when she began to remember the events that occurred earlier. She saw in her mind's eye the cascading droplets of ocean spray and the beautiful sunset, but then her memory became a little spotty.

She thought perhaps she had a dream, that she was on an ancient boat and the sky was dark and stormy. The waves tossed the ship as if it were nothing on the ocean swells and she was drenched to the skin in seawater. Then she could see Solaus taking her in his arms, his skin burning hot as he pressed against her cold body and protected her from the storm. She wanted to melt inside him, to be a part of him completely.

With a longing sigh, she pushed the covers below her waist and sat up in bed. The skin on the back of her head felt like it was pulled tight, and she had an impressive headache. Her sigh turned into a frown and she wasn't sure if she approved of the rather bulky, concealing nightgown she wore.

An empty chair sat next to her bed, and as she ran her fingers through her hair to smooth it, she felt the gash and the stitches. Memory flooded back into her mind and she was momentarily overwhelmed by the images of the rocks and the waves as they cascaded violently over her. She remembered a lantern and reaching out a desperate hand.

With another sigh, she lay back on her pillow and closed her eyes. She surely must have dreamed of Solaus, of his passionate kiss as his arms crushed her to him possessively. She thought if she could just sleep a little longer, she might continue the dream.

Drifting off was more difficult than she imagined as she began to hear the sound of voices echoing through the corridor outside her room. Her door was partially open and allowed the robust laughter to filter through and into her range of hearing.

The laughter seemed strangely familiar to her, but so out of place in the fortress that she was forced to peel back the covers once again and swing her legs over the side of the bed. As she stood, a wave of dizziness engulfed her and she reached out a hand to brace herself on one of the bedposts. The dizziness was gone in a moment and her curiosity got her feet moving in the direction of the doorway.

The hall was slightly drafty and her feet were bare, but she could see the light spilling from an open door just down the corridor. It was easy to tell the voices were coming from there. Her hands brushed against the stone wall as she made her way to the opening, the tips of her fingers tingling from the friction. In moments she was close enough to make out what they were saying.

"I wish I could have seen the looks on those grave robbers' faces when they discovered I had switched the ancient scrolls in that case with an old rolled-up Chinese horoscope I found at the supermarket earlier," an energetic voice boasted and was answered by another raucous round of laughter.

Completely confused, Kaitlin wandered directly into the room where she found Hestor, Mark'het and Drosk playing a hot game of poker and drinking something in a decanter she didn't dare guess at.

The spry historian saw her first and jumped from his seat, his cards spilling all over the table.

"A full house!" Mark'het exclaimed before he noticed Kaitlin standing in the doorway.

"Hestor?" she asked with a shaky voice as they all turned to stare at her. "Is this another dream?"

"Kaitlin, you should not be out of bed," her friend scolded her, immediately coming to her side and wrapping a skinny yet deceptively strong arm around her waist. In just a few seconds, all three men hovered over her and she swatted them away as gently as possible.

"I'm not an invalid," she started to complain, but then looked down at her bare feet and the bedclothes covering her numerous cuts and bruises. "Well, maybe a little infirm?"

Drosk left her to Hestor and said to Mark'het, "I will bring Lilly if you want to get Solaus here."

"I'm surprised he wasn't sitting on the bed next to her the moment she awoke," Hestor remarked jokingly, though there was a slight hint of jealousy in his voice.

"What do you mean?" Kaitlin was perplexed and tried to recall any memory of his presence since her dream by the rocks.

"He means," Mark'het explained with a grin, "that you called his name so many times as you slept away your injuries, he just stopped leaving the room so he could be by your side if you woke and needed him."

Kaitlin's eyes grew wide and she was unable halt the deepening flush that spread from the base of her neck to her cheeks.

"Hmph," Hestor grumbled, propelling her down the hall. "She is obviously still delirious and must be put back to bed."

He cast a stubborn look over his shoulder as the brothers went the other way.

"Can you believe it, Kaitlin?" her old friend chatted excitedly as he sat her back on the bed and pulled the covers up to her knees. "That man you met at the airport—he is the man everyone is talking about, the one you saw at the doctor's office as well."

"Actually, Hestor, I'm having a hard time believing any of this," she murmured as he fussed over her and tucked more pillows behind her back. "He willingly let you come to the island?"

"I did not know where I was going." His eyes twinkled. "But I knew I had to come. I brought Doctor David and he fixed you up. I told that man he had better let me stay on the island and watch out for you. That way, his secret will not get out."

"That man?" she inquired, a little confused by his rapid explanation as she tried to take it all in.

"You know," he answered stubbornly, unwilling to state the name of their host. "That man, the one with the treasure that Nigel always talked about."

At the mention of Nigel's name, a cold wave of dread swept up her spine and caused an uncontrollable shiver.

"Hestor," she said urgently, swiftly taking his busy hands in her own to still him. "You haven't told Nigel anything, have you? Please tell me if he knows about this place or these people who have been so kind to me."

He was immediately taken aback by her urgent plea and sought to comfort her as much as he could.

"Oh, Lovely One," he began as if he were trying to find a gentle way to explain. "I have not seen Nigel since I translated that first part of the scroll for you. I gave him a copy of my initial findings and he went mad as he read on it. He came back to me later that evening, almost desperate, begging for me to disclose your location to him. Of course, I had no idea where you were and he left me with the feeling he was quite distraught."

"And you've heard nothing of him since?"

"Nothing from him. Though I did hear a rumor or two on the street that he had taken up with some rather—" He paused, looking for the right word. "Unsavory characters."

"Until I can be sure of the situation, I think it would be a great idea if we didn't mention Nigel or the amulet, and I do the job Solaus hired me to do," Kaitlin decided and looked to her friend for agreement.

"That is fine with me," Hestor answered her amiably. He patted the pocket of his jacket and removed a deck of cards. "I have already made a few dollars as it is from those friends of yours. I needed a paid vacation anyway."

"You're a dear companion." Kaitlin smiled and slid down her wall of pillows to slip underneath the blankets.

"You do your thing with the camera, and I will continue with the translation of the scroll, as I have brought it with me." Hestor took the topmost blanket and pulled it up to her shoulders. "Oh," he added with a renewed burst of energy. "Did you see that exquisite water clock on the terrace? I hope to persuade Miss Lilly to tell me all about it while I am here."

"I'll be happy to do that," a kind voice said from the doorway.

Hestor turned to see the dark-haired beauty as she regarded Kaitlin's semi-conscious state on the bed.

"I think she may be in need of rest. If you would care to follow me to the terrace, perhaps we can tell tall tales of adventure and history over a glass of wine."

"Did you hear that?" Hestor whispered quite loudly to Kaitlin who had pulled the covers over her mouth to hide her grin. "I have a date. Try not to be very jealous, Lovely One."

"I'll do my best, Hestor," she murmured as her eyes closed on their own.

The silence in the room comforted her aching head. Judging from the sunlight through her small window, it was early afternoon at the latest, so she reasoned she'd have time to take a little nap before the day passed her by.

Knowing Hestor was nearby made all the difference in the world to her state of mind and she felt a great deal safer with a familiar friend on hand to talk to.

She must have drifted off to sleep, because she was startled when she felt the tentative touch of hesitant fingers stroking her hair. Her eyes flew open in a panic, but when she saw Solaus gazing down on her with such a tender look in his eyes, her heart beat even faster.

He immediately withdrew his hand and sat upright in the chair, his face the perfect picture of propriety.

"Lilly said we should let you rest," he explained quickly. "I thought it would be a good idea to bring you something to drink in the event you woke with a thirst and discovered more urges to stroll about the house in your nightgown."

She held back an urge to smile at his veiled attempt to express concern for her wellbeing, and though her head still throbbed she struggled to sit up in bed. Before she could rise more than a few inches he was on his feet, his strong arms around her shoulders as he easily lifted her into an upright position. His body radiated heat, which spilled off him as her face pressed to his chest for a moment.

Kaitlin lost her breath to the desire that flooded her veins, possessing her very soul. She felt an ache deep inside, almost painful, driven by her overwhelming need to be close to him.

Still bent over, he reached his right hand around to capture a down-filled pillow, which he gently slipped behind her back. When the pillow was in place, he turned his hand over so that the small of her back was cradled in his palm as he leaned her carefully into position.

His heart beat like thunder in his chest as she kept her cheek pressed against him for as long as possible. Slowly, he slid his supporting hand up her spine, stopping briefly between her shoulder blades before he withdrew.

Solaus didn't take the seat next to her again, but stood with his long legs spread slightly apart, his hands clasped behind his back. His strong jaw betrayed a line of tension with the effort of his restraint as his eyes held hers with a blazing intensity.

Kaitlin was helplessly overwhelmed by her desire for the dangerously handsome man standing next to her and she longed to ask him if her memory of his passionate kiss was a dream or if it had been reality.

Her rapidly rising pulse pounded through her veins as the blood rose to color her pale cheeks. She tried to control her breathing and looked into his deep blue eyes, but that throbbing pulse pushed against her skull, reinforcing the ache caused by the injury.

Kaitlin raised her hand for one breathless moment, passing her cool fingers over her eyes in an effort to soothe the pain. The look on her visitor's face instantly changed to concern as he reached a gentle hand forward to touch her forehead.

"I should have listened to Lilly and let you rest." The remorse in his voice was clear and the sincerity of it surprised Kaitlin. "Your doctor friend left something for you in case you had pain when you woke, and I can see I have caused you unnecessary stress."

There were so many things Kaitlin wanted to tell him, so many ways she wanted to show him how much it meant to her that he'd come, but her impaired thoughts didn't seem willing to produce the words she longed to say. Instead, she allowed him to give her the medication set out by Doctor Hollinger.

The medicine had an immediate effect on her perception, and everything grew hazy and soft as her eyelids became heavy. She was aware that Solaus had tucked her into a comfortable position and as he put the final touches on the plush comforter around her shoulders, she reached out unsteady hands and took his fingers into her grasp.

"I wanted to see you last night," she said to him, trying to express herself through the haze of sleep taking hold of her system.

"See me?" he asked, not withdrawing his hands as he leaned closer to understand.

"For dinner." She smiled peacefully. "I had a nice dress."

Though Kaitlin didn't see it, his smile at her comment could have lit her heart for years to come. He lightly pressed his lips to her forehead.

"I wish for you to have sweet dreams," he whispered, and didn't let go of her touch until he was certain she was asleep.

•

Kaitlin stood next to the water clock displayed upon an elaborately carved stone platform in one of the relaxation rooms of the temple.

"This is a nice dream," she stated out loud, knowing perfectly well she was asleep and this was a likely by-product of her medication. The visions she experienced since coming into contact with the medallion felt very much like waking dreams to her. After her arrival on the island, they resembled reality so strongly that she often wondered which perception she actually existed in afterwards.

The clock itself seemed identical to the one on the terrace, and she decided it was no wonder that she dreamed of it, considering the focus everyone placed on it since she'd arrived. She looked down at her clothing and saw she wore deep blue silk robes with golden thread embroidered along the hem and the sleeves. She shivered when she recognized the symbols stitched there—the very same icons that emblazoned the tunic of the Prince and marked her as his personal servant.

Kaitlin knew she was dreaming yet she completely identified with the woman she became during these visions and gave herself over to the experience willingly, as she did every time. She felt so strongly that she belonged here.

Determined that she would see as much as she could before the vision was over, she walked to a nearby window. The sun was bright and hot on her face and it took a moment for her eyes to adjust to the light.

The window was on the ground floor and she viewed an open courtyard with tall pillars lining a walkway that stretched as far as her eyes could see. A fountain stood to one side, circular in its makeup, and its center sported several hand carved lotus blossoms as delicate as to appear real, from which clear blue water flowed into the main reservoir.

The scene was so peaceful, so enchanting that she felt comfortable, and without a second thought, raised her hand to release the veil over her face so that the sun could touch all of her skin and warm it.

The contrast of the cool shade on her back and the warm light before her caused her to shiver, and she noticed a shimmering peal of delicate bells from her garment as she did so.

The sound of sandals approaching on the stone was obvious, and she knew the person behind her didn't wish for her to be startled. She smiled to herself as a delicious wave of weakness flowed over her body. It wasn't a second longer before strong hands touched her shoulders to firmly turn her around.

Solaus didn't release her once she faced him, a fact that made her knees shake and threaten to allow her legs to fold. His passionate blue eyes widened at the sight of her naked face, and the very knowledge that he had gazed upon her forced the breath from her lungs and her legs did buckle then.

He captured her with both arms, pressing her against his chest as he gazed into her eyes. Kaitlin's delicate lips parted in an effort to catch her breath and Solaus snapped in that instant, his mouth possessively taking her own with a kiss that sealed both of their destinies forever.

•

"Are you sure you feel up to this?" Lilly questioned her once more as she gently pulled a brush through Kaitlin's unruly hair, avoiding the tender spot on her scalp where the rock had gashed her skin.

Despite her injuries and the painful ordeal she'd gone through the night before, she glowed with excitement and Lilly couldn't ignore the sparkle she saw in her eyes. How well she knew that look, for it was very similar to her own gaze whenever she thought about her husband.

"Wild horses couldn't drag me away." Kaitlin laughed at the old cliché, never realizing how true it could be until now.

"Before you do anything, have a few crackers and see how that works out for you." Lilly gestured to the plate she'd put next to the bed earlier. "There's no use in sending you down for dinner if you cannot eat dinner."

Food was the furthest thing from Kaitlin's mind at the moment, but she nibbled on a dry, salty wheat square in case it might settle her nervous stomach.

She walked with unsteady legs across the room and pushed the shutters open. It was nearly dark outside and a strong ocean breeze flowed over her as she breathed deeply. The familiar ominous clouds on the horizon sent a shiver up her spine and she knew just how quickly the storm could blow across the sea and engulf them.

Lilly clucked her disapproval as the stubborn patient stood directly in the path of the cool night air regarding the bruised twilight sky.

It was true that Kaitlin felt light-headed, but she couldn't be certain of the cause. The salty chill in the air brought her senses to the surface and her skin was alive to the touch of the rough breeze.

With unswerving resolve, she turned to reach for the lovely white satin gown Lilly had gifted her earlier. It had been hung conveniently on the outside of the wardrobe door, as if someone knew it wouldn't stay inside for long.

The light in the washroom was dim, but it mattered very little to her at that moment. She gazed with longing at the hot water Lilly had drawn for her in the porcelain claw-foot tub just a short while before as she assisted her with her hair.

Kaitlin carefully hung the dress next to the mirror and reached down to touch the inviting water. It steamed and as she gracefully ran her hand in a circular motion, the rich oils in the water swirled in iridescent, artistic patterns that drew her gaze in a hypnotic manner.

Suddenly eager to feel the soothing touch of the water, she slipped off the heavy white nightgown and her undergarments. With a steady hand balancing her, she slid one long shapely leg into the tub. It felt like heaven and she gracefully sank down into the sweetly scented bath.

Her hair was tied up on top of her head with a colorful scarf that Lilly had produced while working through her tangles, so she leaned her head back along the cool, white edge of the bathtub. The tiny nicks and cuts she'd received from her tumble along the rocks burned a little at first, but something in the water seemed to soothe her skin.

She ran her fingers along the length of her body, so slick and supple from the oils, and imagined the strong, insistent touch of her rescuer's hands after he saved her from the lashing storm. A deep, physical ache welled inside her and she knew then what true desire felt like, how such passion could consume a person in every facet of their body and soul.

Kaitlin took advantage of the sensual environment and allowed her newly awakened senses to explore the imagined possibilities of her private time with Solaus for dinner. A combination of anticipation and the cooling water of her haven worked to convince her that she needed to rise and prepare herself for the evening, but she still wished she could linger with her fantasy a little longer. While she couldn't be sure the object of her passion felt the same for her in reality, she was quite certain he did in her dreams, and that was a great deal safer against rejection.

With a sigh of resignation, she rose from the bath and reached for the thick, plush towel that hung nearby. After gently drying, she was pleased to discover her skin was fragrant and silky soft to the touch.

Kaitlin slipped on a pair of white satin panties and delicately stepped into a pair of silver, low-heeled sandals. She removed the elegant dress from the hanger and let it fall over her head and shoulders; it conformed to her curves as if it had been made for her.

After she released her hair and it spilled down her back in thick glossy curls, she looked like a silver screen starlet in the mirror. She cast about the room for another light to discover a set of candles on a shelf near the washbasin. Once lit, the candles radiated with a soft, yellow glow near the mirror and did a lot to illuminate the small room.

Kaitlin lightly ran a sheer, silver eye shadow across the top of her lids and followed with a touch of mascara. She'd been blessed with long thick eyelashes, but they were light blonde and not noticeable unless she drew attention to them. She ended with a frosty red on her full lips.

She exited the bathroom apprehensively, both excited yet fearful of her evening to come. Lilly's wheelchair faced away from her, and the woman sat quietly in front of the low burning fireplace. Kaitlin made an obvious sound behind her, and Lilly spun her chair around to greet her.

"Oh, you look so incredible," Lilly said with deep sincerity, an almost wistful look on her face. "I don't think Solaus has a chance."

"Lilly!" Kaitlin exclaimed, and wondered if her desire for Solaus was as obvious to everyone else as it was to the perceptive woman in the chair before her.

Before Lilly could answer, a solid knock came at the door and she resumed a serious look.

"It must be Drosk," Lilly said. "He's come to fetch you for dinner."

She maneuvered close to the door and opened it. Solaus stood directly before her, his strong arms easily supporting a large platter laden with several dishes. He gave her a charming look as he smiled almost bashfully.

"I thought perhaps the patient might be better off taking dinner in her quarters this evening," he explained, his deep voice husky with an undefined emotion.

"Well," Lilly began, "I just never really thought of that. How clever of you, Mister Solaus!"

"I'm told I have my moments." He smiled fondly at the woman who made way for him to enter the room. He automatically looked to the bed as he assumed Kaitlin would be resting there.

"Where has she gotten to now?"

He turned to Lilly once more and spied Kaitlin standing just outside of the washroom. The warm, yellow glow of the candles lit her figure from behind and cast her in a soft and seductive hue as she stared silently, amazed by the kindness of his gesture.

His hands briefly trembled at the sight of her, causing the plates to clink together in an unnerving manner. Lilly quickly made her way to the small table next to the fireplace and cleared it off so that he could put the tray down. She waited expectantly, but neither Solaus nor Kaitlin moved a muscle, their eyes locked in a heated exchange that required no words.

The tension in the room was thick and hot. Lilly fidgeted a little uncomfortably and after a few moments of silence, nudged

Solaus abruptly in the side with her elbow. He started and seemed to finally realize she was present.

With a small gesture, Lilly indicated the table where the dinner tray should have been residing. As he carefully sat the appealing array of food near the fire, another short rap came from the open doorway and Drosk entered with a fine bottle of wine and two crystal goblets.

Lilly cast a quick look of amazement in Drosk's direction and he nodded back at her swiftly as if to say, "I told you so."

"This is the last bottle of your favorite merlot, Miss Kaitlin," Drosk informed her casually. "But Mark'het will be heading to the mainland in the morning. He will bring back more supplies and necessities such as your vintage, I promise."

"How do you know what my favorite vintage is?" Kaitlin found her voice, though her eyes still belonged to Solaus and she didn't have the will to turn them away.

"Your friend Hestor seems to know all your likes and dislikes." Lilly smiled in her direction.

"Indeed," Solaus agreed with a wry look on his face. "He talks of little else. You are planning on entertaining him this evening, Lilly, please?" He finally turned his gaze from Kaitlin and awarded Lilly with a look subtle desperation.

"With your permission, I think we can throw a relic or two in his path to distract him." Drosk laughed, though a little nervous at the prospect.

To the surprise of everyone present, Solaus took a ring of keys from his pocket and tossed them to his companion without a moment's hesitation.

"Show him the whole thing if it takes all night," he stated easily, as if he hadn't just turned over the keys to the greatest treasure ever discovered in modern times.

Lilly raised an eyebrow to her husband who was clearly shaken by the trust bestowed in him. Drosk looked briefly to the beautiful woman in silver and white across the room and knew for a fact that love had no price too high.

As the two men exchanged a nod of understanding, Kaitlin watched Solaus with interest. His presence of character was strong and defining, but his easy, sultry stance in his black pants filled her with a renewed desire. Lost in speculation, she barely noticed her companions leave the room until he turned his full attention to her once again.

With his head slightly inclined, he looked up at her in a shy manner and smiled at her openly and honestly for the first time since she'd met him. Her heart melted at that instant and ran through her veins to fill every part of her body. He took a few swift strides across the room and held his hand out to her palm up. The touch of his skin on hers left an electric shock that stunned and forced her breath to start once more.

She gazed into his eyes, their color brought out by the cobalt colored shirt he wore so handsomely, and strolled across the room with him as if it were a grand palatial procession.

He seated her with great care in the only chair next to the fire. A brief look around the area showed him a stool, which he pulled to Kaitlin's feet and settled upon.

"I did not know what you liked, so Drosk offered to make a little bit of everything," he said, pulling the covers off the dishes, some hot and some cold.

"You must thank Drosk for the effort he's made here."

"I made these." He held out a silver dish filled with red, plump strawberries, a small reservoir of powdered sugar nestled at its center.

Kaitlin nodded and watched as he lifted the swollen red fruit from the bowl. He raised the tip to his lips and gently plunged it into his mouth. It emerged sparkling wet and he proceeded to dip it in the sugar. He held it out to her, just out of reach, so she had to lean forward and capture it. Her lips closed over the sweet tip and she ran her tongue along the bottom to pull it firmly inside.

"Is that good?" he whispered as she swallowed the plump, juicy pulp.

She simply nodded, and he realized it had been a very long time since she'd eaten and her body was probably starved for food. Solaus reprimanded himself once more for putting his desire before her needs and resolved to care properly for his guest.

Kaitlin was disappointed as he backed away and prepared her a small plate of food, but her stomach didn't disagree with his actions and she was forced to admit she was famished.

Though he'd poured them each a glass of wine, neither touched the alcohol. Kaitlin focused on the delicious offering at the table and Solaus was completely caught up by the grace of her movements and delighted by the furtive glances she stole his way.

"What do we have for dessert?" she asked, and Solaus hesitated for only a moment before he answered.

"I can have nothing sweeter than your presence before me." He seemed so serious that she didn't know how to respond before he added, "But you can have cheesecake."

With a grand flourish, he whipped the silver dome off the heavenly confection and tilted his head in inquiry.

A frightening flash of lightning lit the blackened sky beyond her window, briefly casting her room in a stark white light. Despite herself, Kaitlin gasped in surprise and remembered the storm clouds she'd seen on the distant horizon earlier. The electric bulbs in her room flicked and grew dim as she looked around in alarm at the thunder that was forced to follow.

"We often lose the lights when a storm blows in," Solaus reassured her, standing. "It is not uncommon in the least. The fire is low, but I can have it burning bright in a very short time if you give me a chance."

"I don't doubt that," Kaitlin whispered under her breath as she watched him bend over the fireplace, setting two bundles of wood into the low blaze. She noticed many times since her arrival that there were never logs of wood, just tight bundles of something that might be dried reeds, but burned quite well.

The storm sent a second round of light and sound to assault the little fortress, and this time the shutters banged hard against the prevailing wind outside her window.

A moment of panic drove Kaitlin to her feet, though she knew it was a reaction caused by her experience during the last storm. She quickly crossed the room to reach outside and secure the shutters. The cold rain swept across her upper body in a sharp wave and she thought the storm must be fully upon them now. The lightning cracked once more, followed instantly by the thunder, and her suspicions were confirmed.

Though she would have counted the electric lights as dim, they left a noticeable absence of light when they cut off altogether. She turned in the darkness to the only source of illumination available. Her satin gown had grown cold from the rough rain that cut through the window, and the gown brushed against her sensitive skin.

Solaus rested easily in his signature stance, arms crossed and legs spread before the blazing fire. His eyes passed over her shivering figure in the shadows and this time he did nothing to hide the desire there. Kaitlin approached him, drawn by the heat of the fire but terrified by the longing that drove her forward by sheer need alone.

She stood inches away from his shadow and reached forward a trembling hand. With a hesitant gesture, she slipped her fingers inside the crook of his crossed arm to touch his hand buried deep inside. In one brief moment, she stepped forward and laid her head upon his chest, pulling back almost instantly.

Solaus didn't relinquish his grasp on her fingers, and she was forced to remain only an arm's length away from this overpowering figure of a man.

"Come back here," he whispered, his exotic voice filled with wonder and desire.

Before she could consent to his request, he pulled her to him and she instinctively looked up at his face.

She parted her lips to speak, to say everything she'd waited to say to him, but they were past that now. Solaus captured her breath with his mouth and drew it deeply inside as he savored the intent of her unformed words.

Kaitlin surrendered as his strong arms encircled her satin clad figure. Solaus tasted her lips with his tongue, with his mouth, devouring her very essence as he probed the depths of her being. His strong hands stroked her skin with a hungry passion that had been denied for far too long, and he held her lower body firmly against his pressing desire.

"Kaitlin?" He pushed her name out between ardent kisses, suffering from the very contact his lips lost against hers to speak one word.

"Yes," she answered every question he could have asked, as simply as she could.

At her open response, he lifted her as easily as one might hold a feather and carried her to the bed, his lips never leaving hers.

Solaus took a deep, steadying breath and laid her out on top of the blankets. Backing away, he looked into her fire-lit eyes as he stripped off his deep blue shirt.

Kaitlin's lips were swollen by his kisses, and she said once again as he stood in all his sculpted glory next to her bed, "Yes."

With a gentle motion, he reverently lay next to her and waited to be sure. Kaitlin turned to face him, her hands running down his naked back and thrilling at the touch of his skin. He found her lips once more and kissed her with such fervent passion that she though he might consume her.

The ache inside Kaitlin pulsed with an intense need and she slid her right leg between his muscular thighs, pressing against him as her hands tried to strip the remaining clothing from his lower body.

Driven mad by his need for this beauty at his side, he gasped at her urgent movement and allowed her to remove the last of his garments. As she felt his hot, tight skin against her upper thigh, he pulled the strap of her gown off her left shoulder, his hungry mouth searching to pleasure her in other ways.

Kaitlin moaned with abandon and pulled him on top of her. She could feel his desire and knew he needed her as desperately as she needed him.

"I must have you." His voice was laden with lust as his mouth continued to rain kisses upon her breast.

"I am yours—forever." The words were torn from her lips, saying what they both already knew and he needed to hear.

Solaus raised his face to regard her, and saw into her heart. With a tender kiss, he pushed deeply inside her very soul.

The heavens saw their union and marked them once more for eternity.

Chapter Eight

The shutters remained closed from the storm, but the sunlight venting through the slats indicated that the danger was past and the night far behind.

Kaitlin's entire body tingled with the memory of her lover's passionate touch. She'd fallen asleep sometime in the early hours before dawn, though she'd struggled hard to stay awake for fear it would all be a dream yet again.

Not daring to open her eyes, she felt the space next to her on the bed. When her hesitant exploration revealed nothing but cold sheets and a vacant pillow, she forced open her eyelids and prepared to meet the disappointing reality of another fantasy, though it had seemed far more real than any of the others.

Countless blue and white lotus petals surrounded her and she knew then that last night had been no dream, no vision, but the culmination of everything she had dared to hope for since she stepped off the plane in Cairo.

With a sigh of complete satisfaction, she rolled over to lay her head on the pillow adjacent to her own. His scent still lingered on the fabric and she breathed him in as the silky flower petals clung to her glowing skin. There was no part of her body he hadn't touched, no need he hadn't fulfilled as he brought their souls together in a meeting that encompassed the beginning and end of time as the universe knew it.

On the bedside table, Solaus had left her the silver bowl of ripe strawberries, and it reminded her of his sweet kisses the evening before. She gingerly took one, lightly glazed with the juice of its fellow occupants after sitting in the bowl overnight. Distractedly, she ran the soft fruit over her tender lips, swollen from the passionate attention they'd received just hours before.

Kaitlin had a sudden and overwhelming desire to hear the sound of his voice. She pushed the strawberry fully into her mouth and its delicate flesh burst open inside with flavor. As she strolled across the room and opened the shutters she longed to be near him, but she was also thankful for the time alone. She needed to pull her thoughts together and prepare herself to see him again.

The bright sunshine and warm breeze blowing through the window kept her spirits lifted as she drew water into the bathtub and carefully began the process of washing her hair. She could barely keep a steady focus on any of her actions. Each touch on her skin, every sweet scented oil with which she came in contact, brought her mind back to the previous evening.

With conscientious fingers, Kaitlin arranged the satin gown on a hanger inside the wardrobe, laughing to herself at the care she took. Yesterday the gown didn't know such gentle treatment to be sure.

She pulled on a soft, thin white T-shirt, which she hoped highlighted her impressive curves but didn't hint to anyone else of her nearly irrepressible passions. Matched with low-rise, hip hugging jeans and a pair of sandals, she unknowingly radiated her newly awakened sensuality with every movement.

Freeing her wet hair from the towel and allowing it curl down her back, she left the room and went in search of Solaus.

"You are just in time for lunch." Lilly smiled as Kaitlin came out onto the terrace. With surprise, Kaitlin realized the sun was overhead in the post-storm sky.

"I didn't even think to look at my watch," she mused out loud, and noticed the smile exchanged by Drosk and his wife.

"Solaus mentioned to us that you had a rather active evening, with the storm coming on as it did," she continued "He thought we should let you wake on your own today, as he decided to go to shore with Mark'het once the sea settled at dawn."

"Is that what the kids are calling it these days?" Drosk grinned mischievously as he observed Kaitlin's rapidly flushing cheeks. Mercifully, though, he decided to change the subject.

"He mentioned to us he had something very important to do in Cairo, but that I was to assist you with your work this afternoon until he returned."

Though Kaitlin was terribly disappointed by his absence, the thought that he trusted her with the first set of artifacts while he was away thrilled her and let her know she stood in high regard with him after everything they shared. Just as she took the seat Drosk so gallantly offered at the table, she heard an excited shuffling of sandals hurrying through the kitchen and onto the terrace.

"There you are, Lovely One!" Hestor rushed to her side, planting an exuberant kiss on her still warm cheek. In the same motion, he pulled out the empty chair next to her and sat in it swiftly.

"You would not believe the night I had! That man, he allowed Lilly to show me many artifacts and her personal catalog of them. We were up all night and I must say I have never seen such an uncharted collection in my life."

Kaitlin laughed at his oblique reference to Solaus and shot Lilly an appreciative smile. She could only imagine that the saint of a woman, along with her husband, had an entire evening of such references and more.

Lilly acknowledged her look with a brief nod, but Kaitlin knew that Hestor and the former librarian were two peas in a pod when it came to history and they surely enjoyed each other's company.

"Is that the scroll you needed help with?" Lilly asked politely, and Kaitlin turned in time to notice Hestor shift a little uncomfortably in his chair, an inconspicuous roll of parchment tucked under his arm.

"Is that the scroll your colleague loaned you?" Kaitlin raised an eyebrow of inquiry as she faced him, her eyes wide.

"The one about the Persian prince, correct?" Lilly added innocently, digging his hole a little deeper for him.

"Well," Hestor began, gesturing broadly as he conjured many likely scenarios in his mind before he finally settled. "She showed me hers first?"

Kaitlin regarded his innocent look with a mild sense of humor. She knew after such a wondrous show last evening, Hestor would be desperate to produce something impressive of his own, and that legend would have to be it. A deep part of her spirit longed to share the secret of the medallion with Lilly, and perhaps Hestor had unwittingly provided an acceptable segue.

"Then you two can start while Drosk and I get ready in the display room," she finally said.

Her impromptu assistant jumped out of his seat, more than eager to see her skill in action. "It is just a scroll," Hestor spoke softly, laying a hand on her arm as she rose to leave, his affection for her clearly written on his face.

"Soon, my dear friend, I hope it won't matter," she answered. He cast an intrigued look her way but she was already out the door and preparing to encounter her first real session with the relics.

•

"Here they are," Drosk breathed softly as he exited the mysterious door adjacent to the room where her equipment was set up. He cautiously held out two large black velvet satchels as he made his way to the table.

"It's funny," he commented as he loosened the strings pulled tightly around the opening of the first bag. "Out of all the artifacts on this find, he spends the most time with the two of these."

In a smooth and graceful movement, he removed the initial item, an ornate hair comb, and laid it gently on the small box set up under the direct lights and flash equipment.

The relic seemed so familiar to Kaitlin and she hardly dared to breathe as she looked to Drosk with a question.

"May I touch it?" she asked nervously, and he nodded as though he might have anticipated that request.

The teeth of the comb appeared to be made of carved bone or ivory, and they curved out in a four-inch arc. The band itself was gilded with silver and gold, but it was the exquisitely etched carnelian stonework that captured her gaze, each stone hand-crafted with the lifelike design of a majestic and unique sea nymph. The detail was astonishing and with such minute attention, she felt the familiar warmth of passion color her face once more as she gazed upon all their natural attributes.

"And this," Drosk added gently, this time holding the second piece out to her directly.

Kaitlin was amazed at the hand mirror he offered, a perfect match to the delicate comb. The handle was gilded with the same pattern of precious metals, but one breathtaking carnelian the size of a man's fist rested on the back of the oval opposite of the glass. Sculpted upon this soft and rare gemstone was a lovely mermaid.

Surely a queen, Kaitlin thought to herself, astonished by the lifelike carving of the masterpiece. She could feel that the cool glass was intact on the opposite side, and that very fact alone made it a rare treasure to behold.

"I came upon him one night, so very late," Drosk confided to her in a trusting tone. "Of course the electricity had gone in a storm, as always happens here. But the torches in the hall were lit and the ancient pitch burned brightly. At first I thought someone had broken in to the reserve to take our treasure, but then I saw it was Mister Solaus. He sat at this very table and held the mirror the way you do now, but I thought he was gazing into the glass. When I came inside, I saw his eyes were closed."

Kaitlin had subconsciously turned the hand mirror so that the glass could show her face as her friend spoke. She closed her eyes as he continued his tale, trying to imagine Solaus sitting there holding this item so tenderly.

"When I asked him if everything was alright, he opened his eyes and regarded me with the deepest look of hope I have ever seen in a man. If the eyes are the windows of the soul, he is an ancient being, I say."

Kaitlin opened her own eyes to respond, but for a split second she regarded a beautiful, veiled face in the glass. With a gasp, her fingers reflexively let go of the treasure, but thankfully, Drosk was ready for any mishap and caught the gilded artifact before it crashed to the table.

"Are you feeling alright, Miss Kaitlin?" he inquired as he carefully set the mirror on the display box next to the comb.

"I must still be a little dizzy from the accident," she hastily explained the apparition away. "Head injury, you know?"

Her friend nodded in understanding and began to arrange the two pieces in an effort to display them both to the best advantage.

Feeling like she had nothing to lose at that point, Kaitlin drew a deep breath and turned to face Drosk.

"I wonder if you might answer a question for me."

She initiated the conversation harmlessly enough and he smiled his assent.

Encouraged, she continued. "I've often heard the story of how you saved Solaus at the site of the shipwreck, though no one will tell me what happened exactly. I hear you're the one to grant me an audience for this tale."

Drosk stiffened before he could catch himself, and straightened to his full height to look at her curiously.

"And Solaus himself asked you to come to me with this?" he asked, unwilling to give out any information before she responded.

"He did say to me that it was a tale for you to tell." She smiled with total honesty.

"There is not a lot to tell, I would say," he began cautiously.

She nodded at him to continue, hoping his dramatic personality would take over and afford her some insight into the situation.

"When Sol was discovered alongside the ancient wreck, no one considered him to be much of a threat—probably just a washed-up sailor or failed treasure hunter, like all of us." He looked sad then, but raised his chin and continued on.

"It was novel at first, how much he knew about the artifacts. Everyone could see that right away. After a while, they realized he knew too much and might even have a stake in the claim for the property. They chained him up in the bowels of the recovery vessel."

Kaitlin put a comforting hand on his shoulder and knew how painful this part of the tale had to be for him. With a reassuring squeeze, she encouraged him to go on.

"The way they treated him was inhumane. Cruel." Drosk took a moment to recover his voice. "I did not sign on for that. Some of the other men felt the same way, and they left the expedition. It's difficult to tell what they made off with, but it didn't matter much to me. I could not leave him in that hold to die."

A tear slipped from Kaitlin's eye before she could stop its progress, and she knew the treatment he received by the first people he encountered upon his first memory must have been the basis of his cold and guarded demeanor when he met others for the first time.

"Late one night, when everyone was asleep on the ship that

had anchored near the cave, I slipped down into the hull." He regarded her gravely, as if daring her to disbelieve what came next.

"He was unconscious, but I took a hacksaw from the tool shop and I spent an hour grinding through the metal that bound his wrists. He came awake then, and looked at me with those knowing eyes as if he had the answer for every question in the universe. I won't tell you I wasn't scared to death," he said to her truthfully.

"I looked him right in the eye as I freed him from those bonds and I said 'I wish everyone on this boat would just disappear and we could sail away from here with all your treasure.' He replied to me with one sentence only. He said, 'Is that your true wish?'"

Kaitlin breathed carefully, not wanting to disrupt the strange tale she was being afforded, and nodded for him to continue.

"I said, 'Yes, of course!' thinking what else could I possibly want at that moment. With a serene smile on his face, he nodded and stood. I thought he must be mad but he boldly walked out onto the deck!"

He stopped speaking and reached one long arm behind him to secure the back of a chair, which he pulled to the side. "I'm going to sit down now," he said to Kaitlin as if it were the natural course of things for the afternoon.

"Yes, do," she said immediately, concern in her voice as she noticed the color drain from his face leaving him with an ashy pallor.

"He walked onto the deck because everyone on that ship was gone and he knew it," Drosk stated finally, setting his face in his hands. "I never saw any of them again."

Kaitlin's mind instantly generated a hundred reasons why no one was on that ship, and considered selecting one to comfort the brave man sitting in front of her. But she knew he would see through it. He had been there, after all.

"You did the right thing." She said the only words that reflected the truth, and he looked up at her with pleading eyes.

"When the time comes, Miss Kaitlin, I beg of you to do the right thing too." The cryptic words hung in the air and they both knew the conversation was over.

●

Shadows drifted across the windowsill of the display room like the stream flowing through the cylinder of the water clock, but no one noticed the passing of present time, lost as they were in the past and the history of the objects before them.

Drosk turned out to be a natural with the lighting meter, and an invaluable assistant as Kaitlin did her best to capture the intricate details of the craftsmanship on the stunning items.

The sun sank low behind the horizon and though neither visually observed the departure of the outside light source, Drosk commented on the inner environment.

"We are going to need additional exterior illumination," he murmured almost offhandedly. Just as she began to mentally measure the necessary light boost and its placement, Hestor came through the door carrying an ocean breeze with him.

"Mark'het is back from the mainland," he declared importantly, and Kaitlin shivered at the thought of seeing Solaus once more. With a free arm, he passed a small box to her. "These are the supplies you thought you'd need."

She quickly pilfered through the film and developer as Drosk came to stand before her. After only a moment of hesitation, he gestured for Kaitlin to hold out her hand. When she did, he deposited the ring of keys entrusted to him by Solaus the evening before.

"I am very late for fixing dinner." He laughed as if he had a great secret. "I have no doubt my wife is in the kitchen this very moment taking up my slack. I am sure you will see our friend long before I do, so I ask that you return these to him."

Kaitlin's fingers closed over the warm metal as she considered the responsibility. After realizing it gave her the perfect excuse to seek out Solaus, she nodded to her assistant, releasing him from his duties as she found what she was looking for in the box.

"Finally, more indoor film." She laughed and wondered what had made her think she'd only need an outdoor exposure for this expedition. Hestor remained behind as Drosk left the rapidly darkening room.

With strong fingers, Kaitlin popped the top off the special 35 mm film and prepared to retrieve the cartridge. An instant look of surprise drew Hestor's attention when she withdrew a small folded piece of paper instead. As if by force, she read the paper aloud.

•

My dear Kaitlin,

By now you must think me a boorish fool for releasing your affections, as well as the safety of the medallion, to an untrustworthy rogue such as the one you have surely encountered on this assignment.

If I could travel back in time to change the mistakes I have made in the past, you would not be reading this letter. But if you give me just one chance, I can prove to you that my love has no bounds and with your willing support, I will demonstrate for you that my intentions are beyond that of anything you have ever known. Please, allow me to show you the depths of my desire. I have risked everything to discover your location through dangerous and reckless means and I beg of you to secure the key to the iron grate below the keep and meet me at midnight, on this very night.

I remain your ever well-wisher,
Nigel

•

Kaitlin glanced at Hestor, her face the perfect picture of surprise. He merely shrugged as if the letter explained Nigel's state of mind perfectly and he'd already disregarded its contents.

"You don't have anything to say?" she asked him incredulously, and he returned her gaze with a comforting hand on her shoulder.

"I will give you the same advice I always keep on hand regarding our English friend," he answered her firmly. "He never does anything that will not ultimately benefit himself in the end. It is possible he does not truly know of this location, but if he has discovered it, I am sure the price was very high."

"He passed the medallion on to me, Hestor, and the smallest part of me feels as if I should return it to him." She bit her lip in contemplation, then carried out the rest of her thought. "But I'm aware of the way Solaus reacts to these artifacts—the passion they inspire in him is very well known. I can't deny the fact that the medallion must surely belong to him, perhaps even be a part of his past that will help him remember."

"And help you remember as well, I daresay." Hestor chuckled fondly as he produced the antiquated scroll and rolled it out onto the table next to the mirror and comb. "Strange thing about this legend," he began nonchalantly, laying a tattered book of notes next to the manuscript. "Lilly even commented on the striking resemblance between Solaus and the ancient prince in this text."

Kaitlin didn't miss the fact that Hestor finally uttered the name of his rival in her presence, and was charmed by his teasing reference to the legendary prince.

"Certainly," she agreed amiably. "I've always liked older men, you know. He'd be what, a handful of a thousand years old by now?"

"He *is* rather well preserved," Hestor was forced to admit, as he assisted her in gathering up the two items she had been photographing.

Once the items were bagged, she lifted them carefully and entered the small, vault-like room where the remaining relics were kept. Everything was sealed in airtight crates with no markings at all on the outside boxes to indicate their contents.

Solaus must know where each and every item is by heart, she thought to herself as she approached the only box with the top off. It was empty, and she knew this was the place to return her items.

She laughed a little nervously at the idea she considered them *her* items for just a moment, and realized how much these things meant to her. Being near these treasures made her feel as if she shared the secret and mysterious side of this man who had awakened such desire in her life.

As she closed the heavy door between the vault and the studio and turned the key to secure the priceless collection, Hestor crossed the room and gave her a comforting hug.

"I am not worried, Lovely One." He looked meaningfully into her eyes. "I know you will make the right decision when the time comes."

Kaitlin nodded at his familiar sentiment, and he left her in the display room, alone with her thoughts. Absentmindedly, she slipped her hand into the front pocket of her jeans and felt the smooth letter, folded and nestled discreetly inside.

If anyone had asked her what she wanted in a mate before she left on this assignment, the charming Englishman would have fit the bill. But now, after the time she had spent with Solaus, she knew no other man could ever fill her heart or satisfy the passionate destiny he had inspired deep within her soul.

With a light step and no regret, she walked to her room where she retrieved the medallion. It was hot to the touch as it was so often, but didn't burn as she held it tightly to her chest.

"I wish you were the key to his memory," she whispered to the amulet, and a sweltering wave of dizziness washed over her. "And I think it's time we found out if you are."

As the engulfing heat passed and the room returned to normal temperature, she reached inside the wardrobe for a light jacket. She fondly ran her hand over the soft satin fabric of the gown as she lingered over a personal memory of the evening before.

With a decisive motion, she pocketed both the amulet and the keys and made her way to west wing of the fortress where she knew Solaus's office was. She counted her steps when she grew near, trying to calm her nerves as she stroked the surface of the medallion. So many things passed through her mind as she approached the solid wood door, a million different ways to tell him how she came to be in the position she was in.

"I'll just tell him the truth." She breathed deeply and pressed her hand against the door to knock. To her surprise, it swung inward on completely silent hinges and she saw Solaus bent over a sturdy oak desk along the far wall.

He turned toward her the moment she entered, and the look on his face couldn't have been more vividly stunned than if she'd slapped him. Kaitlin knew something was terribly wrong and took a few quick steps to try to cover the distance between them. Without a word, he held out his hand as if to halt her progress. The muscles along his jaw line clenched and she saw the white grip of his fingers on an unmarked envelope.

"I believed you," he whispered quietly, as if afraid his voice would betray him. "You really are very good. I honestly thought you loved me and wanted me more than anything in the world."

His eyes didn't leave hers for one moment as he spoke, and she saw the naked pain he was unable to hide. With trembling hands, his breath labored, he reached inside the opened envelope and pulled out the pictures Lucien had set up for him. He tossed them carelessly on the desk, never breaking eye contact with her as his emotions intensified.

Kaitlin tore her gaze from his tortured hold and saw the evidence lying on the desk. With a gasp of astonishment, she rushed forward and grabbed the pictures. Memories flooded back from the night she'd had dinner with Nigel and her cheeks flamed with embarrassment.

"I was forced to retain a lawyer on the mainland who assisted me in turning over a few of the less valuable items in the find to generate income so I could do what I needed to do here. He is the one who recommended you. When Drosk informed me that a few of the hunters on the expedition had gone away before we escaped, like your friend in the photo," he continued in a monotonous tone, "I hired the lawyer to keep tabs on them to be sure we were safe here."

He reached forward and took the pictures from her grasp and a look that almost resembled jealousy passed across his face for just an instant.

"These are mine," he stated coldly, putting them back in the envelope. "You are not."

"I'm so sorry." The words came from her mouth unbidden before she could formulate her thoughts.

He nodded to her abruptly and turned his face away.

"I know this looks awful, but it isn't what it seems. Please let me explain." She desperately reached out a hand and laid it on his arm as she stumbled over the words she wanted to say.

He visibly stiffened and her touch appeared to cause him an excruciating amount of pain. He spun around to face her once more, this time anger blazing in his eyes.

"I have lost a lot more than my time and my dreams. I have lost a lot more than the safe haven I created here for the people who cared for me," he ground out bitterly.

Tears streamed down her face when she realized she may have unintentionally put Lilly and Develin in harm's way.

"I have lost my faith in you," he stated with finality, and the words fell to the floor like heavy stones on a funeral cairn.

She nodded to him in understanding, the back of her throat

burning too painfully to allow her to plea her case. With all thoughts of the medallion and the letter gone, she turned and placed her hand over her mouth to cover the sob that was about to escape. Without casting a single look back, she left his study and ran to her rooms.

•

"At least take a sip of this tea," Hestor stood next to her bedside, holding out a steaming cup of liquid.

Kaitlin didn't respond to his offer and lay prone on the four-poster bed in the same exact position where she collapsed hours before.

"Lilly is very concerned for you." Hestor attempted to pressure her into taking a swallow. "She said this will calm you and clear your head a little."

"I don't deserve it," Kaitlin groaned miserably, thinking of Lilly's trusting, beautiful face and the unconditional friendship she'd offered her. The tears began to flow once more, though she had no idea what secret reservoir they could be coming from because she should have been devoid of all fluids quite some time ago.

"Perhaps you will feel better if you talk about it." Her friend sat on the edge of the bed. "At least that is what I hear on the TV these days."

"He knows about Nigel," Kaitlin sniffled, and pressed her hands to her swollen eyes as she curled up into a ball on the bed.

"Well, yes," Hestor reasoned out loud. "You went straight to tell him everything when he returned this afternoon, did you not?"

"Someone beat me to it," she said sourly and took a few moments to explain the pictures and the situation that led up to them.

"Nigel is a bit of a ladies man, isn't he?" her friend mused, and then realized he wasn't helping the situation much.

"Of course Solaus couldn't trust a word I said to him after

those photographs came to light," she said inconsolably. "And I don't blame him."

"Give him a chance, Kaitlin. Perhaps with time he will see that you played no part in the conspiracy that surrounds him." Hestor stood and pulled a free blanket from the foot of the bed over her.

"I can't stay here, Hestor," she said in a daze. "I can't bear to see the look of pain in his eyes one more time, knowing I was the cause."

"I have a feeling that even if you truly did wish to leave, no one will take you off the island for such an offense." He patted her on the back. "Like you said to me before—do the job you came here to do. I firmly believe Fate will handle the rest."

"I'll swim away if I have to," she stated resolutely from beneath the blanket.

"Remember the rocks, Lovely One?" His gentle reminder sent a shiver up her spine and she did remember the rocks, then. Only she also remembered the strong hands that rescued her and the hot skin of his body against hers.

The tears came once more and Hestor sighed to witness her in such agony. He crossed the room and pulled the shutters closed against the night air that swirled around the fortification before he left her in peace.

She must have slept for a short time, because she rolled over without realizing it and came up against an uncomfortable bulge in her jeans. She swiftly pulled out the warm, metal keys and everything that happened earlier came back with heart-sinking clarity. She removed the note from her pocket and read it over once more.

Of course! she thought to herself.

If Nigel wanted so desperately to be with her, he could take her off the island at the very least. The sooner she was gone and no longer darkening their doorstep, the better off everyone would be. If he really had the feelings for her that he claimed, she could convince him to leave with her tonight and no one would be the wiser.

She slipped the jacket from her shoulders, the weight of the medallion pulling it down between her fingers. She hung it evenly on the back of the chair with the hope Nigel wouldn't think to take it and it could become part of the collection once again.

She took off her sandals so her progress down the maze of stone corridors would be totally silent, and picked up the weak electric lamp Mark'het had left for her on that first night.

She almost wished she didn't have the keys as she blindly longed for any opportunity to stay close to Solaus, even if he despised her. She shook her head at the thought she considered selfish and knew the quickest way to ease the pain for him would be to disappear from his presence as soon as possible.

She came down the last set of stone stairs and up to the iron grate that was locked tight. She sat the lantern down on the floor of the small space and brought her watch out of her pocket.

It was nearly midnight and her nervous heart beat like it was trying to get away. She momentarily reconsidered her actions, panicked and turned to put the keys back in her pants when a small boat, barely visible in the shadows, drifted up to the small platform on the other side of the grate. The waves beneath the wooden planks rolled in giant swells, lifting and lowering the vessel beyond her vision.

She held the lantern high but it did very little to illuminate the cavern, only serving to bring the menacing pockets of unknown darkness to life so that her imagination could conjure things to lurk there.

The tall and graceful figure of a man leapt from the pitching water craft and landed deftly on the dock, barely hesitating to tie off as he rushed forward to the iron bars.

"I knew you'd be waiting for me," Nigel said breathlessly. He reached his right hand through the grate, stroking the pallid skin on her face.

She closed her eyes for one moment, trying to invoke some type of response to his touch, some little bit of feeling for this man in front of her. It was no use. The only thing she saw was the passionate blue eyes of her stormy lover.

"Do you have the key?" Nigel hastily interrupted her thoughts and Kaitlin produced them automatically without thinking. Before she could even consider opening the gate, he plucked the key ring from her fingers and found the proper key. In another moment he was through and held her in a sudden embrace. She froze at his touch, but he didn't seem to notice her unusual reaction as he covered her face with tiny kisses.

"Where is the medallion?" he questioned her immediately upon his release of the embrace, and she felt a little disoriented by his rapid attentions.

"I don't have it on me, if that's what you mean," she stammered in reply, unsure of what to say.

He actually appeared angry for a slight moment, but then he softened his demeanor and smiled at her in understanding.

"Of course," he said as if the idea just occurred to him. "You would keep it in a safe place until I came for it. I understand."

"Did you come for it, or did you come for me?" she asked.

He noticed her tenseness right away and his whole appearance shifted once more to become the perfect image of a man in love.

"For you, Kaitlin." He sounded sincere enough that she almost believed him. "Shall we just get your things and be on our way?"

With a hesitant gesture, she reached for the lantern and began to walk up the stairs. She didn't notice Nigel's last-minute look over his shoulder at the boat he tied to the dock, or the quick nod he issued to the second figure perched easily along the prow. It was much too dark for her to have seen, but her imagination was not far off at all—there were monsters in the shadows.

She reluctantly slowed her pace as they neared her quarters, and each step she took was filled with apprehension. Everything about what she was doing felt wrong. She thought perhaps Hestor was correct; maybe she should have stayed a little longer. Maybe she should have done anything except what she was doing right then.

The door was closed exactly as she left it, and she had no reason to believe anyone would be inside. Kaitlin briefly considered slipping into the room and slamming the door behind her, barring Nigel from entering, but there was no way she could leave him free to roam around the island fort and cause possible harm to her friends.

She opened the door a few inches and motioned for Nigel to enter and followed directly behind, trying desperately to come up with a way to make this right. What she saw when she entered the room turned the blood in her veins to ice water.

Solaus sat easily in the chair next to the fireplace where they had shared their passionate evening just one night before. He'd draped her jacket over his left arm and from his right hand swung the medallion.

"Looking for this?" he stated casually, smiling at her as though nothing had transpired between them that afternoon. She felt Nigel's hand wrap around her upper arm and squeeze it almost painfully, but she truthfully could feel nothing but those blue eyes as they searched her own.

"I remember everything." He snapped the chain of the amulet as the disc fell squarely into his palm. "I am Djinn. For centuries I roamed the world with this cursed amulet upon my neck, never to be removed by my hand or that of another. And for those centuries no man nor god knew the suffering I endured from the torment of my lost love."

He spoke directly to Kaitlin now and swirling visions of the temple surfaced at his words. She forgot Nigel was in the room at all until he spoke.

"Cursed amulet," the intruder breathed in wonder. "With the

power of the immortal world around your neck, you felt nothing but the lament of lost love?"

"Love was my greatest treasure," he answered the Englishman, as if it should be so obvious. "When the forces of nature removed the talisman from my neck in a great cataclysm, I was happy to drift away, lose my immortality and die. But the magic of the medallion had permeated my being for so many countless years that it kept me alive, aware of the world and dreaming in a state of suspension."

Kaitlin was overwhelmed by the truth of his story and the knowledge that they belonged together. The very distance in the room between them was thick with destiny and she began to pull away from Nigel who only tightened his hold on her.

"And then you discovered me," Solaus finished, nodding to the wild-eyed adventurer. "But more importantly, you discovered the medallion. When you removed it from my presence in the sand, I awoke but with no memory. And though the magic still lingered in my veins, I became mortal again."

Nigel looked with a hungry passion on the medallion Solaus cradled, and seemed to burst into action all at once. He grabbed Kaitlin from behind, his left arm wrapped around her neck. His right hand produced a wicked looking dagger, which he shoved up against her back, right above her kidney.

"I knew the legend was true when Hestor showed me the beginning translations," he practically raved in elation. "What a fool I was. I had the medallion in my grasp and I sent it away for the promise of mere trinkets!"

Kaitlin gasped with pain as she tried to twist out of his grip, shocked by his behavior and surprised at the strength in which he was able to pin her.

"You don't want to do this, Nigel." Solaus rose carefully and held out one placating hand. "You are not that man—the one who would hurt his friends to forward his own gain."

"Do you really want to take that chance?" he smoothly asked Solaus, pressing the knife's point just a fraction of an inch deeper into Kaitlin's skin.

Solaus immediately took a step forward, unable to repress the urge to protect her. The sharp point caused her to stiffen and he instantly halted his advance.

"The way I see it is this," Nigel began, and for all his madness, sounded perfectly reasonable. "You value love over power. If you truly love Kaitlin, you'll give me the amulet and save her beautiful life. I am willing to part with her for the promise of immortality, but I doubt you will find much happiness in your future plagued by visions of her dead at your feet."

"He won't hurt me, Solaus," she pleaded with the man across the room. "Please don't give up your heritage, your whole world, to save me."

"You are my world," he answered simply, and without another passing moment, tossed the medallion into the air. Nigel artfully grabbed it as it came near, releasing his hold on her neck. She was frozen, unable to believe the sacrifice Solaus had just made for her. She remained as she was, standing up against the desperate treasure hunter.

"Kaitlin, I wish you only the best." Nigel urged her toward the fireplace with a gentle prod, breaking her countenance.

She stumbled toward her love and as she grew near, he held out his arms. She collapsed against his chest, crying desperate tears of happiness to feel his touch once more.

Solaus didn't spare one look for the amulet that had ruled his immortality as it passed to a new owner. He only had room for a single vision in his sight and that was Kaitlin's face in his hands.

"I swore to myself that if I ever had another chance, I would not lose you again," he whispered against her lips as he kissed her salty tears away. "I cannot condemn any manner that Fate has brought you back to me. I know now that you came as you had to."

"Why compromise?" A cold and sinister voice echoed from the shadows of the doorway.

Kaitlin froze in recognition, a wave of fear paralyzing her body as she turned in slow motion to face the graceful figure of the assassin as he entered.

"Good evening, Dove," he addressed her with real pleasure before turning to face Nigel.

She tried to call out a warning to her misguided friend, but to her amazement, he hailed the newcomer warmly.

"I have what I came for," Nigel told him triumphantly, tossing him the ring of keys she'd used earlier to let him in the keep. "And I'm sure there's enough treasure hidden here to satisfy your needs."

"You don't know what I need." He calmly looked his accessory in the eye as he drew a sleek black gun, fully equipped with a silencer. Before anyone could utter a word of protest, Lucien shot him directly in the chest.

Nigel slumped to the floor. His hand that clutched the amulet relaxed its grip, almost holding it out for the taking.

"One down, one to go," the cold-blooded killer spoke in a simple manner that chilled Kaitlin to her very core.

In a lightning-fast move, Solaus tried to step in front of Kaitlin.

"No!" she cried, knowing perfectly well Lucien wouldn't kill her, but Solaus had just made himself vulnerable.

She immediately moved away from Solaus, hoping to reach the madman in time.

Not the type of person to hesitate, Lucien aimed the gun without comment and fired three bullets into her protector.

Solaus hit the wall with a sharp crack and clasped his wounds. He took his hand away from his chest and to Kaitlin's horror the blood flowed freely as he slid down the wall. As she hovered over

Solaus whose eyes dimmed, the assassin hummed a little tune and strolled over to Nigel's inert figure to reach for the medallion.

"Why?" Kaitlin asked him, her heart breaking with each rattled breath that Solaus took.

"As I said, why compromise? I prefer to have the girl, the treasure and the immortality."

He turned his face to regard her, his hand on the medallion. The moment his attention shifted, Nigel cried out with a great roar of pain and swung the hand with the hidden knife as forcefully as he could in the direction of their attacker. The knife connected with his extended neck, exposed by Kaitlin's innocent question.

A look of amazement passed across Lucien's face and he abruptly stood, releasing the gun and the medallion both as he touched the hilt of the dagger. With one swift movement he pulled it out, exposing the artery Nigel had skillfully punctured.

"Oh," he said casually, fingers dropping the blade. His gaze found Kaitlin's once more. "Goodbye, Dove," he said softly as his body folded to the floor in a slow and graceful spiral that seemed to take an eternity to complete.

Solaus was no longer responsive. Kaitlin stood slowly with her hands lingering on his as long as possible, looking at the blood all around her almost completely in shock.

"Kaitlin, please," Nigel called to her, the life in his voice fading fast. She walked to the area where Lucien had dropped the medallion and picked it up with shaking hands.

"I would have never hurt you," he said with sincerity, and she knew that to be true. She looked to Solaus, then back at her friend on the floor. Neither man would last much longer and she had to make a decision quickly.

Steeling herself as she gripped the magical item tightly, she crossed the distance and knelt before Nigel. Slowly whispering in his ear, she draped the medallion over his neck and walked out of the room without a second glance behind her.

•

Kaitlin stood at the edge of the peaceful terrace, her blood covered hands resting lightly on the rail as the sun bloomed in the distance. The water clock sat next to her, measuring the time and reminding her of a dream she had once, long ago.

She heard the sound of approaching footsteps and smiled as they grew closer. Strong hands settled upon her shoulders and firmly turned her around.

Solaus stood before her, his smile perfect and radiant. Her knees grew weak and she felt them give way underneath her. Solaus was more than happy to catch her in his arms and hold her close against his chest as he covered her mouth with a deep, penetrating kiss.

When she could stand again, he wrapped his arm around her waist and stood with her side-by-side as Nigel emerged onto the terrace.

Kaitlin smiled as she watched him nearly glow with the medallion around his neck, the power he'd always desired flowing through his veins.

"Thank you for my wish." She laughed at the wonder in which Nigel held out his hands, flexing his fingers as if he thought lightning might come out of them.

"Oh, that?" Nigel inclined his head in the direction of her long lost love, disdainfully pretending to brush the blood off his sleeve. "That was *his* wish."

"When I put the medallion on all those centuries ago, I could not bring you back from the dead," Solaus explained to Kaitlin. "So I wished that one day you and I would be together again, far away from the land that brought us so much pain and that we would know the love we were meant to experience all along."

"I twisted it around a little, so that it could work for him." Nigel nodded confidentially at Kaitlin before he continued. "Don't think it was a freebie though. It definitely counted as one of the three wishes that were made."

"All three were spent?" she asked with curiosity, and he raised the medallion off his chest a little to remind her.

"You said the key to his memories, right? I can hear that now, you see."

"Then who had the second wish?" she asked him, trying to remember everything that had happened in the past few days.

"Let me think," he started slowly, and Solaus laughed at the deep amount of concentration the newly appointed Djinn had to expend to trace it back.

"The second wish was made by a child," he finally blurted out. His predecessor nodded with approval. Kaitlin struggled hard to recall all the events that took place, when Drosk entered the courtyard, unashamedly crying, followed by Hestor and Mark'het who ran around the area like a disorganized fire brigade.

Drosk approached Kaitlin and she felt a renewed moment of fear when she remembered Lucien had been on the grounds for a long while before he met his fate in the guest chamber.

Solaus nodded to the weeping man and set a steadying hand on his shoulder. With knowing expectation, he turned his head to get a good view of the doorway leading into the kitchen.

Lilly walked onto the terrace with strong legs, holding her son in her arms and beaming at her husband who shook with great, silent tears of joy.

Kaitlin gasped at the sight of the beautiful woman, her face filled with a serene happiness as she strode confidently across the flagstones to join them.

Nigel coughed a little from the edge of the porch. "That was me, too." He nodded proudly. With a small farewell wave, he began to fade away into the background, but not before he graced her with a saucy wink.

Solaus pulled Kaitlin away from the small group as if he couldn't wait another moment to have her all to himself. With tender and reverent hands, he held her face as if he cradled the greatest treasure in existence.

"I spent an eternity dreaming of your heart next to mine. There was never one moment in all the centuries past that you were unloved by me. I don't think I can ever become weary of gazing into your eyes."

He looked at her with a smoldering fire that took her breath away, as if it were the first time she caught the sultry passion in his gaze. Kaitlin stood on tiptoe and brushed his mouth with a gentle kiss before he could continue.

"I am yours—forever," he added, and his earnest gaze spoke the truth of his words.

"We belong together," she answered him, her smile begging for another touch from his lips. The world seemed to slow around them and Kaitlin couldn't think of anything that could go wrong at this moment.

"He'll be back, you know," Solaus casually referred to Nigel. "He won't know what to do at first."

"Then we can only hope to discover a method in which to send him away."

She teased his lips with her breath and wrapped her arms around his neck.

"Wishes are magic if you have three," he added sagely—and gave in to his desire, fulfilling the promise of passion he held for her in his eyes.

• • •

Kimberly Adkins

Kimberly Adkins resides in Nashville, Tennessee, Music City USA. She is an avid artist who works with oils, acrylics and water colors. She also spends time song writing and sometimes singing—but only when forced! She has always loved Egyptian lore, as well as science fiction and fantasy. For Kimberly, writing romances is a wonderfully appealing outlet for "magic and passion."

www.KimberlyAdkins.com

CAST IN STONE

BY KERRY A. JONES
ISBN: 978-0-9793252-2-9

**He had waited seven hundred years to love her.
She was sworn to destroy him.**

"Do I have a great book for you to read! ...a dazzling paranormal romance that will grab your attention from the first chapter straight through to the last... It's gothic and sexy! "
Julie Kornhausl
Romance Reader at Heart

"If the following books [in the Quinguard Immortals Series] are as good as the first, it will be an excellent series and a must-have for those who believe in soulmates. I for one will never look at gargoyles in quite the same way again."
Janet Davies
Once Upon a Romance

"An extraordinary tale with memorable characters, a fresh premise and solid writing. Ms. Jones crafted a winner."
Janalee Ruschhaupt
Paranormal Romance Reviews

"A riveting tale of love, lust, hate and magic... a must-buy!"
Rosemarie Brungard
Romance at Heart Magazine

www.BlackLyonPublishing.com